BLUEST NIGHT

B ASH

BLUEST NIGHT

Published by BAJ PUBLISHING LLC
Kingfisher, Oklahoma, 73750

ISBN: 979-8-9927541-1-7
LIBRARY OF CONGRESS CONTROL NUMBER:

Printed in the United States

ACKNOWLEDGEMENTS

First, I want to give honor, glory and praise to my Lord and Savior, Jesus Christ.

I want to acknowledge some individuals who supported me during an exceedingly challenging time in my life.

J.D. – J.D., although not my blood brother, became a particularly good close friend. He was my confidant, adviser, and most importantly my brother.

A.F. – A.F., like J.D., was a close friend. She offered advice and support during this tough time. And some of the best baked pastries.

Ward and Glass – This effective team of attorneys believed in me and fought for me, ensuring that justice was served.

LASTLY, THE MOST IMPORTANT PERSON I WANT TO ACKNOWLEDGE:

M.J. – My wife put up with so much during this time. She absolutely saw me at my worst mentally, emotionally, and physically. There were times that I was not nice, however she loved me through them despite fighting the urge to leave. M.J., I love you and I thank God for placing you in my life.

INTRODUCTION

To the law enforcement officers who choose to stay loyal to their oath, THANK YOU.

To the American public who choose to support law enforcement, THANK YOU.

To the American public who choose to resist law enforcement, I UNDERSTAND.

THIS IS POLICE CORRUPTION AT ITS WORST.

WHAT WILL IT TAKE TO STOP IT?

WHO WILL STAND FOR WHAT IS RIGHT?

THIS IS A FICTIONAL BOOK WITH FICTIONAL CHARACTERS AND A FICTIONAL STORYLINE.

NO PARTS OF THIS BOOK SHOULD BE TAKEN AS FACT.

THE STORIES ARE LOOSELY BASED ON THE LAW ENFORCEMENT CAREER OF B. ASH WITH INSPIRED STORIES FROM HIS LONG TIME FRIEND AND COWORKER, J.D.

SOME ARE FICTIONAL STORIES BASED ON TRUE EVENTS. THE CHARACTERS AND DESCRIPTIONS ARE CHANGED TO PRESERVE CASE INTEGRITY AND HUMILITY OF THE PERSONS INVOLVED.

THE STORIES THAT ARE BASED ON TRUE EVENTS ARE EXAGGERATED, HOWEVER AS CLOSE TO THE TRUTH AS POSSIBLE.

**** THIS BOOK IS NOT AND SHALL NOT BE USED AS AN INSTRUMENT FOR ANY TYPE OF ILLEGAL ACTIVITY; NOR DOES IT CONDONE CRIMINAL BEHAVOIR. ALL CRIMES AND/OR SUSPICIOUS ACTIVITY SHOULD BE REPORTED TO THE PROPER AUTHORITIES. ****

LAW ENFORCEMENT OATH

I DO SOLEMNLY SWEAR THAT I WILL BE ALERT AND VIGILANT TO ENFORCE THE CRIMINAL LAWS OF THIS STATE, THAT I WILL NOT BE INFLUENCED IN ANY MATTER ON ACCOUNT OF PERSONAL BIAS OR PREJUDICE.

THAT I WILL FAITHFULLY AND IMPARTIALLY EXECUTE THE DUTIES OF MY OFFICE AS A LAW ENFORCEMENT OFFICER TO THE BEST OF MY SKILL, ABILITIES, AND JUDGMENT.

SO, HELP ME, GOD.

TABLE OF CONTENTS

CHAPTER 1

AT WIT'S END

BOILING POINT POLICE DEPARTMENT

1312 Critical Juncture

P.O. Box 1600

Boiling Point, Louisiana 70098

Phone: 318-555-2345

Fax# 225-555-8765

To: Louis Benoit, Attorney General
Office of the Attorney General
103 Turning Point Road
P.O. Box 15223
Hot Water, Louisiana 70099
Phone: 318-555-1234
RE: Officer Gideon Thibodaux Complaint

Mr. Benoit, pardon my long letter. I pray that you can find time in your busy schedule to read my request.

I am Deputy Chief William Perry of the Boiling Point Police Department in Boiling Point, King County, Louisiana.

I am making a formal request that an investigation be conducted on the City of Boiling Point's heads of department for reasons of official misconduct,

corruption, extortion, embezzlement, money laundering, narcotics crimes, burglary, robbery, assault and battery, and finally murder.

Commissioner Hayes, Chief Anderson, Captain Dupree, Sergeant LeBlanc, and Officer Morgan should all be brought in and questioned by your office and after reading this, you will know why.

On March 24th, 2021, Officer Gideon Thibodaux was suspended without cause. I picked him up from the police department and dropped him off at his house.

I told him to meet me at our friend's house.

Before he got out of my car, Officer Thibodaux handed me a flash drive and told me if anything happened to him, to look at the contents with our group of friends.

I took the flash drive, but I did not take his words to heart.

The flash drive that Officer Thibodaux gave me had incredible information on it. I believe this information will lead us to wherever his body is being kept. Assuming he is deceased.

The drive is too large to send through email; therefore, I am mailing a copy of the flash drive. In the event you do not receive it, I have been discovered and the drive confiscated by the listed names above.

If I come up missing or worse, dead; you know it was by those individuals.

Begin there.

As for the flash drive, Officer Thibodaux kept unbelievably detailed notes, audio recordings, video recordings, photographs, and eyewitness accounts of criminal activity performed by Chief Anderson, Captain Dupree, Lieutenant Menendez, Sergeant LeBlanc, Officer Morgan, and Officer Jacobs.

The witnesses are listed as civilians and other police officers.

Three of the civilians were known drug dealers and have all been murdered.

The following is what happened in the months leading up to March 24th, 2021, and the reason I am requesting your office investigate these departments instead of the District Attorney's Office or Louisiana State Police Bureau of Investigation.

CHAPTER 2

TABITHA JACKSON

Tabitha Jackson was a reporter and Chief Editor of the *Ledger*, a small news article outlet that she owned and ran.

Tabitha moved to Boiling Point three years ago to start her editorial company when the owner of the *Star* retired and sold the business to her.

Tabitha heard that Boiling Point, Louisiana was a bustling city comprised of four major neighborhoods. On all of which she had to keep a keen eye.

Boiling Point had an exceedingly high crime rate and illegal drugs were the center of it all. The fact that legislators legalized the worst of these drugs did not help.

Tabitha was not your average Louisiana small town farm girl. She was tall, with a slim athletic build.

She had her hands full with the number of articles she wrote daily. She had three reporters that worked for her, but the brunt of the work was hers.

Tabitha, being an athlete, was regularly active in the sporting events taking place in Boiling Point.

Not just for reporting purposes, but she coached a little league softball team in the spring and a little league indoor soccer team in the fall. She also practiced mixed martial arts as she had a brown belt in karate and a purple belt in jujitsu.

She was admired by the upper echelon of the city, as she was incredibly smart and authored amazing articles.

However, her deadliest mistake happened when she attracted the attention of the Boiling Point chief of police, Marcus Anderson.

Being skilled in the martial arts, Tabitha knew she could take care of herself, but being educated in hand-to-hand combat may not be good enough to save her.

Tabitha managed to skate by for three years, without running into Chief Anderson.

The Boiling Point Police Department had a Public Information Officer with whom she made contact, any time she needed to speak with someone from the Police Department.

Each week, she entered the police department's P.I.O. office and received a summary report of all the crimes and contact reports the officers made that previous week.

Tabitha became familiar with the Public Information Officer over the course of her three years and felt comfortable and safe with him; that is, until she received an anonymous tip from a concerned citizen.

The tip implicated several officers in illegal activities that included violating federal and state laws.

Tabitha was floored when saw the name of the Public Information Officer, Anthony Peters, on the list.
Although they never really spent much time together, personally, Tabitha felt Officer Peters was someone that could be trusted.

She had interviewed him many times discussing robberies, murders, drug investigations, missing persons, and several other incidents and accidents.

She recalled public speaking events at which Officer Peters attended and spoke.

They shared dinners in the nicest restaurants, and at this moment, Tabitha was relieved that she kept their relationship professional - not only because this information could harm her business, but had she become intimate with Officer Peters, it would have ended her 5-year marriage.

Tabitha's husband, Charles, was a jealous man. He was tall, muscular, and very assertive.

No one messed with Charles, because not only was he intimidating in stature, but he was also a black belt in karate, a three-time black belt champion in Brazilian jujitsu, an instructor of Taekwondo, and a two-time Mr. Olympian.

Charles was older than most of the men Tabitha had dealt with, but he was by far in better shape and more good-looking.

Tabitha knew to keep the information she had received confidential and did not share it with the other reporters.

She felt this information could get a person killed and she had a responsibility to protect her employees.

However, she did not feel safe with the information, so she told Charles as a precaution.

Charles told her that he had a couple friends at the police department whom he trusted, and he would ask them to help protect her. Then, he cautiously asked if their names were on the list.

Tabitha frantically searched the list up and down three or four times and did not see their names.

She let out a long sigh of relief.

Tabitha had never met or even heard of the two officers Charles mentioned; however, if he trusted them, she would have no choice but to trust them, also.

She had just been given damaging information that could bring down the highest-level members of the Boiling Point Police Department, one of which she considered a valued friend.

For purposes of validity, Tabitha needed to begin looking into the information she had received.

CHAPTER 3

CHIEF ANDERSON

Chief Marcus Anderson was used to getting his way; that is how he grew to become the chief of police.

Chief Anderson cheated his way from patrol officer to assistant chief in a short amount of time. He was a good-looking man and knew how to manipulate anyone. He had the entire city fooled.

The few people who challenged him found out just how menacing he could be and backed down without saying a word.

As for the rest of the citizens, they had no clue.

Chief Anderson became chief by a unanimous decision during a commissioner's council meeting four years ago.

Everyone thought it was a great idea after seeing how hard he had worked during the absence of the previous chief.

Chief Anderson bit his tongue and swallowed his pride to get what he desired the most: the power.

He was a working administrative assistant chief, meaning he managed the day-to-day administrative tasks of the department, but he also responded to calls of service and worked other shifts when they were short officers.

While the council decided of whom the next chief of police would be, Assistant Chief Anderson played his best cards.

Without permission of the current chief, Commissioner, or Commissioner's Council, Assistant Chief Anderson hosted fundraisers inside the police department, and with the help of the police department's human resource officer, he created a program identified as the Reformed Opportunity Council.

The R.O.C. was explained as an opportunistic approach to help the communities by bringing in summer events for the youth, reading programs in the schools and public libraries, and even donations for Christmas toy-drives.

From the outside, the R.O.C. seemed like a safe, legit nonprofit organization, and people from all over sent in donations.

But the R.O.C. was a ruse. Assistant Chief Anderson was using the money for his own personal gain. In fact, the R.O.C. was not a registered nonprofit organization at all.

Assistant Chief Anderson felt like he was soaring in the clouds as high-end people noticed him, paying for lunch meetings, and coming into the Police Department to spend time with him.

However, he was drawing too much attention.

Marcus Anderson did not know four years ago, but he was headed toward a whirlwind of a downward spiral. His biggest downfall was becoming Chief of Police.

Or did it just speed up the inevitable?

During an executive session in the Commissioner's Council Chambers, Assistant Chief Anderson was appointed the position of Chief of Police.

Once the gavel slammed signifying the change in command, members of the Police Department noticed a sadistic smile on Chief Anderson's face.

A few of the officers in the crowd began to whisper to each other, questioning the decision.

There was a department meeting following the Council meeting where the entire police department, with its eighty-five employees, gathered in the large two-story training room to congratulate the new chief.

A small crew of disapproving officers arrived but did not take part in the celebration.

Their actions did not go unnoticed. Chief Anderson approached the group and asked why they were not celebrating with him.

One officer responded crudely, saying, "We were just observing. We have been on calls all evening and just stopped in between them."

Chief Anderson looked displeased with the answer and replied, "Didn't I see you all at the meeting?" The officer again responded by saying, "We were there. We left to respond to a burglary alarm, and now we are back."

This answer settled Chief Anderson, although he was becoming cautious of the group.

He decided to separate the officers who did not show acceptance of his new role in the department.

He kept some of the officers on nights and moved other officers, the ones he wanted to closely watch, to the dayshift.

Chief Anderson knew who he could trust to follow his orders without question, and he appointed them to supervisory positions despite their lack of law enforcement knowledge or tenure in the police department.

He also hired officers who were closely related to him which brought division between himself and other officers who once believed he was right for the job.

These officers began to question his leadership and spoke with the group of officers that were openly against Chief Anderson.

Chief Anderson decided he did not need an assistant chief because he had a ranking system in place; however, due to there always being an assistant chief, the Commissioner's Council forced him to appoint one.

Commissioner Hayes opened the position to an application process for anyone in the Boiling Point Police Department who had ten years of experience or more, which was more experience than Chief Anderson had.

The Council would review the applications and appoint the best applicant for the position.

They chose William Perry.

Displeased with the decision, Chief Anderson changed the name of the title from 'Assistant Chief' to 'Deputy Chief.' He felt it was a disgrace to the title, however William Perry was elated and respected the position.

The Department was already heading toward a catastrophic demise.

The officers who were against the Chief, worked extremely hard to serve and protect the City of Boiling Point, Louisiana under Deputy Chief Perry's supervision, while Chief Anderson and the other supervisors lived a lavish life on duty, ignoring calls for service and using their uniform to disgrace their marital status.

These supervisors believed themselves to be untouchable because they had had affairs with top members of the municipal leadership who now could not discipline them because of their atrocious behavior.

However, there was still the group of officers that upheld their law enforcement oath, ethics, and moral turpitude.

Over the course of four years, these officers had denounced Chief Anderson and reported him to the Commissioner, District Attorney, and even the Louisiana State Police for investigation.

It came down to one officer, who wrote a perfect timeline of the events as they occurred. This officer presented photographs, audio recordings, and written reports to the Commissioner.

Little did he know, the Commissioner supplied all the evidence, built to bring Chief Anderson off his high horse, directly to the chief.

The Commissioner attached a note on the file that stated,

"You have a problem in your department that needs to be dealt with."

The Commissioner then removed himself from having any contact with officers that had not been addressed by a supervisor.

This only encouraged Chief Anderson and the supervisors under him to continue their corrupt behavior. And they would take it too far.

CHAPTER 4

GIDEON THIBODAUX

Tabitha needed to infiltrate the police department to get more information on the officers listed in the anonymous tip. She approached Chief Anderson with a proposition to conduct a ride along to gain access to the department's secured facility.

Chief Anderson decided to allow the reporter to ride along with an officer for three weeks. And he chose himself as the chauffeur. This was his chance to finally make his move on the beautiful young woman.

Chief Anderson told Tabitha when they would begin and where to meet.

She was extremely uncomfortable with the idea of being near Chief Anderson because his name was at the top of the list, and he made her feel gross.

Tabitha decided to oppose Chief Anderson's decision and requested another officer in rebuttal. This did not sit well with Chief Anderson, as he was not used to being told no, and he refused to allow her to ride along with any officer.

Tabitha had to go about this an unusual way. She needed to be inquisitive and think outside of the box.

'How can I get an officer to allow me to ride with him without alerting the chief?' Tabitha thought. Then the idea struck her like a blunt object.

Tabitha spent the next three days in different areas of the city with her radio scanner waiting for the right officer to come along.

On this day, she was in the Watts neighborhood of Boiling Point. That is when she saw an officer chasing a fleeing suspect. "Stop running! I'm catching up to you!" The officer shouted.

The officer caught up with the man and pushed him just above his shoulder blades in the center of his back. The man began to stumble before conducting an acrobatic front roll, scraping his forearms on the graveled asphalt.

The man quickly jumped up and shook the pain in his arms away. Seeing this, Tabitha's first thought was to record the tempered standoff between the officer and irate man.

She heard the officer tell the man "I told you not to make me run. Now, give up!"

The man reached in his pocket but was having a challenging time removing whatever was in there. The officer told him to stop reaching and drew his taser.

The cartridge had already been used during the foot pursuit and he did not have a backup.

The officer quickly jumped into action, holstering his taser, grabbing the man around the shoulders and with a hip toss, he threw him on the ground.

The man's hand flew out of his pocket as his body slammed on the ground.

A glass pipe shattered against the asphalt when the man's hand made a hammering impact. The officer quickly gained control of the man's hands placing them in cuffs.

Seeing that the man was now in custody, Tabitha approached the officer with her camera still recording.

The officer was slightly out of breath and irritatingly asked the man "you ran because of a meth pipe?"

The man said "yeah, fucker. I'm not going to jail with this on me."

Tabitha asked the officer "why is he going to jail?"

The officer replied, "he has several outstanding felony warrants."

Then he picked up the man and with a jerk asked him "and you knew it? That's why you ran."

The man looked at the officer and said "you're just lucky I like you. If you were any of the other pigs, I would have broke your fucking nose."

The officer just shook his head and said "Randy, why do you always do this? You know it's just failure to appear warrants and you'll bond out."

Randy sighed and said "man, G.T., I wish it were that simple this time. I got a revocation on a thirteen-year bid."

The officer hung his head and told Randy "I'm sorry. But I have to take you in for the warrants." They turned and began walking back toward the officer's patrol car.

Tabitha saw the compassion the officer had for Randy and thought 'this must be one of the friends Charles talked about.'

She saw her opportunity to ride with a reputable officer. One that even the criminals had respect for.

She turned off her camera and watched as the officer placed Randy in the back seat of the patrol car.

Then she approached him and asked "I'm a reporter for the Boiling Point Ledger. Can I ride with you?"

The officer looked puzzled and stated "you'll have to fill out a request form and have it approved by a supervisor.

I'll meet you at headquarters when I'm done at the Boiling Point Justice Center, and we can get that form filled out together.

But first I have to write a report on this arrest. Won't take long."

'Finally,' Tabitha thought. She turned and quickly headed back to her car then drove straight to the Watts headquarters of the Boiling Point Police Department where she waited in her car.

The booking process took about thirty minutes for the officers of the Boiling Point Police Department.

Then the inmates were turned over to the Justice Center detention staff.

Randy was treated for minor cuts and scrapes on his forearms and hands where the glass pipe shattered.

The officer eventually arrived at the Watts headquarters and parked in a secured parking lot.

Tabitha saw him pass behind her car that was parked in the public parking lot.

She got out and walked into the front lobby of the headquarters.

The Watts headquarters was the largest of the four neighborhoods that housed a department.

It was also where the top brass, including the P.I.O. and the Chief's offices, were found.

Tabitha did not know all the supervisors and hoped to not see the Chief while she was inside.

He had already denied her permission to ride with any officer other than himself.

She knew how controlling he was based on that one conversation.

Tabitha approached the reception desk and told the heavyset and very well made-up woman sitting behind it that she needed to see an officer for a ride along.

The woman looked up from her computer, and, while rolling her eyes, in a snark tone, replied "which officer?"

'Shit!' Tabitha thought. 'I didn't get his name.'

The woman stared at Tabitha and began tapping her long colorful fingernails on the desk.

"Hello!" the woman annoyingly blurted. "Which officer?"

"G, um... G.T.?" said Tabitha, unsure of her answer.

"G.T.?" the woman replied. "Lady, we don't use initials 'round here. This is a place of p'a'fessionalism."

Tabitha scoffed at the 'PROfessionalism' comment and looked around.

She noticed a directory on the desk and saw the name 'Officer G. Thibodaux' on it with an extension to his phone beside it.

"Thibodaux. Officer Thibodaux," stated Tabitha with a gulp in her throat.

She was incredibly nervous because she had spent too much time in the lobby, and she did not know if or when Chief Anderson would see her.

Just then Officer Thibodaux exited a door to her right and said "oh great, you are here. Come on back."

Tabitha looked at the receptionist and grinned a nervous, yet relieved, smile.

As they entered the patrol room, Officer Thibodaux introduced himself. "Sorry, I didn't catch your name earlier. You work for the Ledger?"

"Yes." Tabitha exclaimed. "Well, I own the Ledger and I'm the editor as well. I'm Tabitha. Tabitha Jackson" she said informatively.

Officer Thibodaux turned toward her and said “oh, that impressive. I’m Officer Gideon Thibodaux.” He spelled it out as if she were writing it down, “T.H.I.B.O.D.A.U.X.” Then he pronounced it “Ti-Buh-Doh”

Tabitha was relieved to hear the name because it was one of the men Charles liked. That meant she was safe.

Tabitha’s eyes widened as she blurted out “that’s unique.”

“Eastern France” said Officer Thibodaux. “But I’m not French. My great, great ancestors were. They settled in Louisiana after the French sold the territory to Thomas Jefferson in 1803.”

Tabitha was amazed by the amount of knowledge Officer Thibodaux had about his surname.

Officer Thibodaux pulled a piece of paper from a basket and began to fill it out. “Sign here” he told Tabitha, pointing to a signature line at the bottom of the page.

“Alright. Let’s see how much trouble you can get in.” he told her. He placed the paper in a basket labeled ‘Request for Approval.’

They headed out the back door to the secure parking lot and climbed into his patrol car.

“Bravo 643, Dispatch.” “Bravo 643, go ‘head.” a robotic sounding voice responded.

Officer Thibodaux requested "show Bravo 643 back in service."

"You know," Tabitha said, "I've never been in a police car."

Officer Thibodaux looked annoyed by the comment. He thought Tabitha was just another woman impressed by the uniform and he did not like that.

Tabitha wanted to know more about Officer Thibodaux. She asked him how long he had worked for the Boiling Point Police Department. "Seventeen years," he said.

Tabitha curiously asked, "how long has Chief Anderson worked for the Department?"

"I don't know. Maybe eight or nine years." Officer Thibodaux answered.

"Why were you passed up for chief? Or did you not want it?" she asked.

Officer Thibodaux drove silently, ignoring the question. "I mean, it just seems that you have more experience than Anderson and you've been here longer." Tabitha hesitantly said. "Why wouldn't you get that position?"

"Look, Ms. Jackson. You do not know me. Don't speak on things you know nothing about." said Officer Thibodaux very matter of fact. Then he asked, "why did you want to ride with me?"

Tabitha stammered in awe of the question. “Well, I asked Anderson for permission to ride with an officer, but he denied my request because I wouldn’t ride with him.” She continued, “I just didn’t feel comfortable.”

Officer Thibodaux motioned his finger toward his lips and said “careful what you say. These cars are wired, and he can hear everything. If he knows you are in my unit, he’s probably listening right now.”

Tabitha’s face turned pale, and she mouthed “oh my god!” Blood rushed to her face. She was instantly embarrassed. “I’m sorry.” she quietly said.

Officer Thibodaux pulled up to a convenience store and they both got out of the car.

Walking toward her, he said “listen. I do not mind you riding with me however, just watch. Any comments you have, either keep them to yourself or you can text me. Otherwise let’s keep it professional. The chief already hates me, but he can’t fire me.”

Officer Thibodaux told Tabitha she could ride with him for the rest of his shift, but he did not feel it safe for her to continue riding. Especially since the Chief already refused. Her actions could be detrimental for them both.

With one arrest in the bag, Officer Thibodaux had eight hours left of his twelve-hour shift. And this was a good night for a reporter to ride in the patrol car.

CHAPTER 5

MINISTERS OF DEATH

Just after dark fell across the city, Officer Thibodaux responded to a murder at a residence owned by the Dupont family. He was second on scene and told Tabitha to stay in the car.

The residence was a brown wood frame single-story, single-family home with red window trim, a black attic vent at the front of the home, and visible basement windows with no trim. The front door was red with a full glass storm door.

When Officer Thibodaux arrived, he saw his partner, through the picture frame window at the front of the house, standing in the middle of the residence with his arms resting on his duty belt. It was unclear what was happening inside the home but dispatch informed Officer Thibodaux that there was a definite murder.

Officer Thibodaux cautiously approached the front of the house, running through the front yard crouched with his service weapon drawn as he climbed the steps of the porch to the front door.

He called for his partner who told him that everything was okay. Unsure, Officer Thibodaux entered the residence with his service weapon still drawn and upon entering the living room, it was clear that the scene was safe.

What Officer Thibodaux saw was his partner standing over a revolver at the feet of a deceased male. Officer Thibodaux's partner told him that the male killed himself. Officer Thibodaux was confused because the call came across as a homicide not a suicide.

He put away his service weapon and moved closer to the body.

Officer Thibodaux asked what his partner needed from him, and he said, "nothing right now." He thought, 'I can secure the weapon for him or guard the body so he can secure the weapon.' He made the request and was given permission to enter his partner's patrol unit to obtain evidence bags and the crime scene camera.

Officer Thibodaux took the camera out of its case and began photographing the residence from the street as he approached the front door. He continued taking pictures as he reached the weapon, photographing the make, model, and caliber.

He retrieved the weapon, making it safe by removing the ammunition and walked out of the residence. He then locked the gun in a lock box found in the trunk of his partner's patrol unit.

Officer Thibodaux walked to the passenger side of his patrol car and told Tabitha that the residence was safe and that she could get out of the car to fulfill her role as a reporter. He then told her to stay out of the yard because it was part of the crime scene.

As Officer Thibodaux was walking back toward the front door, he saw, through the picture frame window in the living room, a man standing in the distance behind his partner.

He rushed into the residence and asked who the man was. His partner told him that a teenage male was in the house, and it was he who called 911.

Officer Thibodaux stepped toward the entryway of the dining room and saw a woman sitting at a desk.

Officer Thibodaux jumped back and removed his service weapon and exclaimed "holy shit, man! Why didn't you tell me someone else was in here!" His partner laughed and said "oh, she's dead too."

Officer Thibodaux was beside himself. He thought the male he saw behind his partner, through the window, could be responsible for murdering both the DuPont couple.

He told his partner "We need to secure that kid. He could be the killer." but his partner just laughed and said, "he's not.

He was on the phone with dispatch when the second shot rang out." 'Doesn't mean he wasn't the shooter' thought Officer Thibodaux.

Officer Thibodaux took the crime scene camera and began to photograph the residence. He began where he left off with the front exterior and moved inside, photographing the entryway, and living room leading up to the body of the male.

Officer Thibodaux took astounding pictures of the entry and exit wounds from the gunshot to the man's head. He thought 'it's amazing that the brain liquifies and oozes out of the skull through a tiny hole.'

But the hole was not tiny, and that thought was quickly interrupted when he heard a raspy voice grumble "ouch, my head."

The hair stood up on the backs of their necks. Goosebumps ran down their bodies. Startled, Officer Thibodaux and his partner turned around and eerily stared at the woman sitting at the computer desk.

They both believed she was dead.

But now she was talking ... and moving.

Officer Thibodaux rushed to her and asked "ma'am! Are you alright?" She did not acknowledge him but only raised her right arm, placing her hand on her head and said "ouch! My head!" in a weak and raspy voice.

Officer Thibodaux grabbed his handheld radio and requested an ambulance to their location advising that there was a live victim who suffered a gunshot wound to the rear left side of the head.

He began taking pictures of her injury, documenting through photography the entry and exit wounds through her blood-soaked hair.

He followed the trajectory of the bullet through a glass champagne flute into the wall opposite her and found the bullet hole.

The bullet was lodged deep inside the hole, and he could not see it.

He checked the other side of the wall where the refrigerator stood but there was not an exit hole. He knew the bullet was inside the wall.

Officer Thibodaux continued to take pictures of the residence and found certificates hanging on the living room wall. The certificates showed that both Mr. and Mrs. Dupont were ordained ministers.

Officer Thibodaux turned and looked at Mr. Dupont's lifeless body and thought 'this guy was a preacher? What could have happened that led a preacher to kill his wife and then himself?'

Just then, the front door flew open, interrupting his thoughts, and a young man entered the residence.

He ran directly toward the deceased male with anger and rage in his flailing body movements and all eagerness to stump on the face of the deceased.

Officer Thibodaux tackled the young man before he reached the nearly decapitated preacher and wrestled with him forcing him out of the house. He questioned him on the front porch.

The young man said that he had recently been discharged from the state penitentiary and arrived at home earlier that day.

He celebrated his return with his parents (mother and step-father), brother and reunited girlfriend. He said that his parents were wine collectors and wanted to celebrate by drinking wine all evening.

They drank and ate bread, cheese, and crackers but the wine proved to be too much for some.

His girlfriend became highly intoxicated and needed to relieve herself. The closest bathroom was inside the parents' bedroom so that is where she went.

After realizing she had been gone for a while, Mr. Dupont decided to go check on her. He found her asleep face down on their bed with her feet hanging off. She was fully clothed but that did not stop Mr. Dupont.

He climbed on top of the bed and mounted the young woman from behind then began to dry hump her. She woke up in a daze, confused about what was happening.

She tried to push him off, but Mr. Dupont was too heavy. The young woman began to squirm and scream, and the commotion grabbed the attention of Mrs. Dupont and her son.

They ran in the room and found the two lying in a compromising position in the bed.

The young man became infuriated and tried to fight his stepdad. Mrs. Dupont told them to leave so he grabbed his girlfriend and left.

Officer Thibodaux informed the man that his younger brother was inside the residence and unharmed. He united the two on the front porch.

It was there that the younger brother informed Officer Thibodaux of what happened next.

Mr. and Mrs. Dupont began to argue. Their youngest son heard the argument but dismissed it thinking it was normal fighting. That is until he heard the first gunshot.

He ran out of his bedroom, through the kitchen and stopped in the entrance to the dining room where he saw his dad standing in the entryway to the living room holding a gun to his head.

Mr. Dupont looked at his son and said, "I killed her. You want to die too?"

The teenager saw his mother's lifeless body sitting in the computer chair and then ran to his room where he called 911. While he was on the phone with the dispatcher, they both heard the final gunshot.

The dispatcher asked what the sound was, and the phone went silent. She panicked and called for his name asking if he was okay. She was relieved when she heard his voice over the phone saying, "my dad just killed himself."

She was saddened for the young man because he just lost both his parents in a horrendous manner but glad that he was alive and well.

While speaking with the brothers, Officer Thibodaux was distracted by green and red lights hovering above the residence. They would come and go, periodically. He looked around and saw Officer Peters' patrol car in the distance.

Officer Peters arrived and began taking pictures of the scene with a drone he had bought through the R.O.C. Its designated purpose was to only be used for department functions; however, Officer Peters created a side business and used the drone for extra cash.

Officer Thibodaux returned to taking pictures of the residence until the first EMT arrived. He showed her where Mrs. Dupont was located and learned quickly that this EMT was not right for the job at hand.

She screamed and yelled "how come she's not dead? She has a giant hole in her head."

Officer Thibodaux asked if she could help Mrs. Dupont and the EMT responded "it's unlikely that she will live. I don't understand why she isn't dead already."

Officer Thibodaux prayed for someone else to arrive and his prayers were answered.

More EMTs and fire rescue showed up. They began searching for a pulse and blood pressure for Mrs. Dupont. They attached her to multiple machines and placed a neck brace on her.

Then they laid her on a vinyl stretcher designed to be carried into tight spaces where a regular stretcher could not fit. All the while Officer Thibodaux stood by taking pictures.

Officer Thibodaux captured the moment the team laid Mrs. Dupont on the stretcher and pieces of her skull fell out of her head. He photographed giant blood clots and brain fragments that fell from her head.

He thought 'there's no way she will survive this.'

Officer Thibodaux remained inside the residence taking pictures until the crime scene unit arrived.

They took over the scene and he directed them by using his photographs to recover both rounds dispensed into the heads of Mr. and Mrs. Dupont to cause their deaths.

One of the rounds was lodged in the wall behind a painting in the dining room. It was the round that ended Mr. Dupont's life.

It was not until the coroner showed up that the residence gained a very paranormal presence. Officer Thibodaux saw wooden windchimes throughout the interior of the residence.

The windchimes began chiming as Mr. Dupont's body was being moved into a body bag. Officer Thibodaux and other officers aided with the removal of the body.

Once the body was removed, the detectives and crime scene unit released the residence from being a crime scene.

CHAPTER 6

GRAND AM

Tabitha had taken several pictures of the scene at the Dupont residence and because she was in the patrol car at the time the call was sent out, she had enough to draft an article in the weekly paper.

Officer Thibodaux walked over to his patrol car and said to Tabitha "let's get you back to headquarters. I have to get these pictures uploaded and write a quick report. I can finish my report when I come back tonight."

Tabitha was exhausted. She had been awake for over 24 hours and just spent the last 9 hours outside the scene of an attempted murder-suicide. She had her own report to write and photos to upload.

"When will I see you again?" Tabitha asked Officer Thibodaux.

"We'll see." he responded as he climbed into the driver seat of his patrol car.

They arrived at the headquarters and Officer Thibodaux parked behind Tabitha's car in the public parking lot.

"Have a good night." Officer Thibodaux said to Tabitha as the sun was rising above the tops of the buildings reaching up to the skyline.

Tabitha looked around and to the sky, and said "night? I don't know if I'll be able to sleep in the daylight." They laughed and he drove away.

That night Officer Thibodaux returned to work after a short sleep. His eyes had heavy dark rings under them, and he was very sluggish.

Entering the office, his sergeant called him into his office.

"You look like shit." the sergeant said in disgust.

Officer Thibodaux explained "Well, I did work four hours over my shift and only slept for five hours. What's up?"

"Chief Anderson is highly pissed with you. Apparently, he did not want a reporter riding with officers, and you let her ride in your patrol car? What were you thinking?" The sergeant tore into Officer Thibodaux.

Clearing the air, Officer Thibodaux said "there were no directives regarding the reporter. I checked my emails and the board for updates and directives. Nothing mentioned the reporter."

Knowing this, the sergeant replied "I know. I already explained that to the Chief. He's giving you a pass this time.

But don't let her back in your car. I don't care if she's hurt, don't put her in your car."

Officer Thibodaux nodded in agreement.

He then walked out of the sergeant's office and headed directly to the coffee station. He poured a full cup of steaming hot black coffee and several packets of pure cane sugar. 'This should wake me up.' thought Officer Thibodaux.

He sat at his desk where he finished his complete report of the attempted homicide/suicide and attached it to the report from the other officers.

Suddenly his radio chimed signaling that EMS and Fire were needed. The dispatcher advised there was a motor vehicle accident involving a pedestrian.

It was just after dark, and the accident was on Marion Road in the southern Watts neighborhood.

Officer Thibodaux responded to the MVA located on the road bordering the neighborhoods of Watts and Gray within the city limits of Boiling Point, Louisiana.

Officer Thibodaux was the first to arrive. As he approached the scene, he saw a vehicle parked in the middle of the eastbound lane with its high beams on and hazard lights flashing.

Officer Thibodaux slowed his patrol car down as he crept around the vehicle. From the front, he saw no damage to the vehicle and no one around it.

The bright lights did not help matters and neither did the glare of the red and blue visor lights bouncing off the hood of his white patrol car.

Officer Thibodaux drove past the vehicle and as he moved to the rear of it, he saw what appeared to be a white male kneeling next to a white female who was lying motionless on the cold asphalt.

He drove about twenty feet or so beyond the rear of the vehicle then turned around and positioned his patrol car partially off the road at an angle so that the emergency lights warned other responding units and travelers.

He turned on his spotlight and directed it toward the pair and the rear of the vehicle to illuminate the scene to the best of his ability.

Officer Thibodaux wanted to be able to view the full scene (if there were any weapons or blood, how severe the injuries were, if any, any damage to the rear of the vehicle, the license plate, make, model and style of vehicle, if there were any other occupants inside the vehicle, and were there any breaking marks on the roadway to indicate the driver attempted to stop prior to striking the pedestrian).

Officer Thibodaux left the warmth of his patrol car and ran to the couple. He asked what happened and the male told him "She just jumped out of the car while I was driving."

Officer Thibodaux could see that the woman was breathing and radioed to dispatch to speed up the ambulance. He asked the man if she hit her head and he said he did not know.

Officer Thibodaux felt that something was not right with this couple and requested additional units from the Gray precinct come to his location.

The accident occurred in the jurisdiction of the Gray precinct therefore the accident needed to be worked by those officers.

Officer Thibodaux responded to the scene of the accident to see where it occurred and if there were any injuries.

He would then report his findings for dispatch to send out the proper medical and traffic units from the correct precinct.

The woman began to wake up and move her arms and legs with agonizing pain. Officer Thibodaux held her hand and told her to keep still. He then ran to his patrol car to get his jacket. He ran back to her and covered her body then rested his knees on the hard road near the top of her head creating a makeshift neck brace so that he could refrain her from moving her neck and causing more damage.

He remained in this position for over forty-five minutes. During that time, another officer arrived and began to process the scene by gathering vehicle and occupant information.

The other officer spoke with the man who turned out to be the driver of the vehicle, a silver 2006 4 door Pontiac Grand Am.

The woman began to panic. Officer Thibodaux assured her that help was on its way. He spoke with her asking if she remembered what happened to her.

She told Officer Thibodaux that they were at a party where her boyfriend got really drunk.

She said that she offered to drive but because it was his car, and he did not feel 'too buzzed' he would drive.

The woman said she did not want to leave with him because she could see that he was entirely too drunk to drive but he forced her into the car.

On the way back into the Watts neighborhood, they argued. She begged and pleaded to get out of the car, but he held onto her left arm.

Because of his drunken state, he could not properly drive the vehicle and began to swerve while driving at a high rate of speed.

He let go of her arm to regain control of the vehicle and stopped in the middle of the street.

She quickly, and out of fear, got out of the vehicle to begin walking back to Watts, all-the-while he was yelling at her from the driver side window.

She did not remember much after that except feeling intense pain in her legs, back, and head then waking up to Officer Thibodaux standing over her.

The evidence at the scene revealed how clear it was that the boyfriend ran her over.

Officer Thibodaux motioned to the other officer on scene to place the male in handcuffs by bumping his wrists together in an "X" shape.

Later, Officer Thibodaux informed the Gray precinct officer that the man was intoxicated, and this accident might have been intentional.

Officer Thibodaux remained on his knees holding her head until the ambulance and fire rescue arrived to take over. He then joined the other officer in obtaining a statement from the boyfriend.

His story changed several times, but he was consistent in saying "she jumped out the car."

They could smell the odor of alcohol on his breath as he spoke and reported as such to the traffic units when they arrived.

The boyfriend tried the field sobriety tests for the officers and was taken to the hospital for a warrantless blood draw to evaluate his blood for illegal intoxicants.

Officer Thibodaux left the scene returning to Watts headquarters.

By the end of his shift, Officer Peters had photos of the scene posted on the department website.

Officer Thibodaux completed his fourth twelve-hour shift and went home on the morning of his first of three days off.

CHAPTER 7

THE REVEAL

While on days off, Officer Thibodaux received a call from Charles, Tabitha's husband.

Charles invited Officer Thibodaux to their house for drinks and to talk about something especially important.

Officer Thibodaux showed up at Charles' house not knowing that Tabitha was his wife. "Gideon!" Charles called out as he opened the front door. "I'm glad you could make it. Please come in. Can I get you anything to drink?"

Officer Thibodaux had never been to their house and was taking in the elegant architecture of the foyer. "No, I'm okay." Officer Thibodaux answered.

Charles responded, offering a list of drinks. "You sure? We have wine, beer, Cokes, water." He then raised his brow and leaned into Officer Thibodaux saying, "the best liquor."

Officer Thibodaux felt he would be disrespectful at this point if he did not drink anything, so he requested water.

Just then, they entered the kitchen where Tabitha was filling a bucket with cubed ice from the freezer. She turned with a smile to greet Charles' friend and quickly lost her smile when she saw it was the officer with whom she had rode.

"Oh, Charles! This is your friend?" Tabitha asked. "Yes." answered Charles. "Gideon, this is my wife, Tabitha." he continued.

Officer Thibodaux did not flinch. "Nice to meet you, Mrs. Jackson." he responded.

Tabitha looked at him in confusion. Why was he acting like he did not know who she was? They spent an entire twelve-hour shift in the same car. She did not like that he was acting this way and spoke up.

"We've met." she answered. "I went on a ride-along with Officer Thibodaux a couple days ago."

Before Charles could respond, Officer Thibodaux joked about Tabitha nearly causing him to lose his job.

Charles was very confused and sat on a bar stool. "You two know each other?" he asked.

Officer Thibodaux responded, "Not very well."

He continued, "We met as I was making an arrest. She asked how to go about riding with an officer and I told her to meet me at HQ. She did not mention that she had previously been forbidden a ride along by the chief. Charles, you know I'm already in hot water with the chief."

Charles glared at Tabitha disappointedly. "Yes, Gideon. I know what all you have gone through at the police department. That is why I asked you to come over tonight."

He took a breath, "You see, Tabitha here received some damning information on a lot of officers and top brass in the department. I told her I had a couple friends on the force that I could count on to protect her should anyone find out she has this information."

Officer Thibodaux looked intently at Charles and Tabitha. "You got the list?" he asked.

Tabitha's head snapped up as she looked into Officer Thibodaux's eyes.

Charles asked him "you know about the list?"

Officer Thibodaux responded, "Who do you think made it?".

He continued, "I have a lot of information on the corrupt officers within the department but after what happened with the complaints I sent to the Commissioner; I know I can't trust anyone on the force."

Officer Thibodaux focused his attention on Tabitha. “I have read some of your articles and I’ve seen how hard you work to bring out the truth. I thought you would be the best person to help me. I didn’t know you were Charles’ wife. Why have I never seen you two together?”

Tabitha answered, “we’re both extremely busy. We have a dinner date every two months or so. But we always are available to have dinner at home together. Except for that twelve-hour shift. Charles understood because there was a murder suicide.

Charles finally broke his silence. “Gideon. What do you expect my wife to do with this information? Why would you put her in such danger? Why wouldn’t you come to me?”

Officer Thibodaux reiterated “I did not know she was your wife. Had I known...”

Tabitha interrupted. “It’s fine, Gideon. Can I call you that now? Gideon?” Officer Thibodaux nodded. “Good.” She responded. “So, we need to make a plan. Charles, you said there were two officers. Who is the second?”

Charles looked at Officer Thibodaux questionably as he answered “William Perry.”

Officer Thibodaux slightly smiled.

Tabitha questioned “the assistant chief? He is not corrupt?” Charles asked her if his name was on the list.

Confused, Tabitha looked at Officer Thibodaux. "Why do you trust him?" she asked.

Officer Thibodaux sighed and answered. "Deputy Chief Perry has been a friend for a long time. He came to me when he found out Chief Anderson was targeting me. He told me to watch my back and gave me some of the information I turned over to the Commissioner."

He continued, "I didn't name any of the references that the information came from so the Commissioner told me he wouldn't accept rumors. I told him to follow the leads himself and he refused."

Swallowing a sip of water; Officer Thibodaux finished his statement, "Then he passed the information to the chief. The chief tried to fire me on the spot, but he couldn't because that falls under the category of retaliation."

Officer Thibodaux advised that although Deputy Chief Perry was someone to trust, he should not be involved unless something very devastating happened.

"What would that be?" Tabitha asked. Officer Thibodaux turned his glance toward Charles and with a straight face he said,

"My death."

CHAPTER 8

BERRY HILL ROAD

His days off went by quickly and before he knew it Officer Thibodaux was gearing up for his first day back on shift.

He entered the Watts headquarters to clock in and grab his body-worn camera then he sat down at his desk.

While waiting for the computer to turn on, Officer Thibodaux realized the shoestring on his right boot had come untied. He leaned down to tie it and saw an obscure object under his desk.

Officer Thibodaux recognized the object at once and became furious although he did not react to it.

Instead, he rose from his chair and walked out of the police department. Officer Thibodaux walked to his patrol car, got in, turned it on, then removed his body-worn camera and exited the car.

He called Deputy Chief Perry on his personal phone but before the line connected, the dispatcher came across the radio.

"Dispatch to Bravo 643." 'Damn it!' thought Officer Thibodaux. He hung up the phone and grabbed his lapel mic. "Go for Bravo 643". The dispatcher informed him "Bravo 643, report to the Pilot Travel Center on Berry Hill Road for reports of shots fired."

Officer Thibodaux jumped in his patrol car and drove directly to the convenience store. On the way, Deputy Chief Perry called him back. "You called?"

"Yeah, but I can't talk now. I'm headed to a shots fired call." Officer Thibodaux retorted.

"Oh damn. You out by yourself?" asked Deputy Chief Perry.

Officer Thibodaux responded "yeah, for now. I should be good though. It's just shots fired, not a shooting."

Deputy Chief Perry assured him "okay. Call if you need anything. Stay safe."

Officer Thibodaux hung up the phone knowing he needed to tell Deputy Chief Perry about what he found under his desk inside the headquarters.

However, he could not do so while around his body-worn camera and dash camera.

The cameras recorded constantly and looped over the recordings after a certain length of time.

And Chief Anderson had access to view the footage when and wherever he wanted.

Officer Thibodaux arrived at the Pilot Travel Center on Berry Hill Road and looked around outside before casually walking into the building.

He saw the workers, all women, inside through the large window huddled near the drink station.

One of the women was an ex-girlfriend of Officer Thibodaux. She had not seen him since she moved back to Boiling Point and was extremely relieved to know it was him that was responding to the call.

When she saw him walk through the front sliding doors, she cried out "thank God you're here. I thought we were going to die today!"

The woman tried her best to wrap her arms around Officer Thibodaux's large torso as she squeezed him in a hug. He scoffed and placed one arm over her shoulder asking what happened.

The other women approached all speaking at once. He quieted them down with the motion of his hands and asked the store manager what happened.

She explained that a group of young adults entered the store and appeared to already be intoxicated.

They were identified as one white woman, one Black woman, and one white man. Another older Black man waited outside the store in a white Lincoln Town Car.

The trio shopped at the store for snacks, energy drinks and beer. As they moved toward the register, a pistol fell out the right pant leg of the man's black pants. One of the women with him bent over to pick it up then slid it into the waistband of her jeans without missing a step.

The cashiers saw the action of her stuffing something into her pants but did not see what it was. They began to question her about what she was 'attempting to steal' and an argument ensued.

Knowing that the gun was in her waistband, the lady began to grab for it. The second woman and the man pulled her out of the store, and they entered the Town Car without paying for the items in their hands.

The town car left the parking lot.

As they drove away, the store employees heard several loud pops then thuds against the building. They realized what was happening and called 911.

Officer Thibodaux arrived at the store within five minutes of receiving the call.

The other employees explained what happened and described the assailants, specifically a girl with green hair.

They told Officer Thibodaux that the girl with the green hair had lots of facial piercings.

The store manager pulled up the store surveillance footage.

They observed the individuals enter the store. The man was wearing a black jacket with black sweatpants and black and white tennis shoes.

One woman was wearing a black jacket and blue jeans while the other woman was wearing a maroon jacket and had blue and green dyed hair.

Officer Thibodaux, and the store employees, witnessed the group walking toward the register where the man made a strange movement with his right leg.

Then the woman with the green hair, walking behind the man, bent over and picked an object up from the floor.

The store manager rewound the footage and pressed play then zoomed in.

When they saw the item on the floor, she paused the tape so Officer Thibodaux could tell what it was, however the video was too pixelated to verify what was on the floor.

All Officer Thibodaux could plainly see was a black object. He told the manager to zoom out some hoping to fix the distorted picture.

The crew of all women were flabbergasted when they observed the object to be a black pistol.

Officer Thibodaux's ex-girlfriend stammered to admit that she argued with the woman believing that she was shoplifting.

She felt nauseous knowing that the "merchandise" the woman was trying to remove from her waistband was actually..., a gun.

She turned around burying her face in Officer Thibodaux's uniformed covered body armor as she wept in disbelief and shame. She exclaimed "I almost died because I judged her!"

It was then clear that the sound they heard was gunshots.

Next, they viewed the surveillance footage of the parking lot to identify the vehicle. Upon seeing it, Officer Thibodaux knew exactly who the driver was.

Geared with the knowledge of who the participants were and that they were armed, Officer Thibodaux went to the address of the vehicle owner.

He found the vehicle in the front yard and saw that the front door was closed. There were several people outside the residence, and it appeared they were having a party.

Because he was working alone, Officer Thibodaux rehearsed in his head how he was going to make an arrest.

"You're going to jail!" No, that won't work. "Uh, hey!" Nope. "Um... excuse me, are you the one... yep, green hair." No, that won't work either. "Just go up there." Officer Thibodaux confidently rehearsed aloud while looking in the mirror.

He casually walked through the front yard speaking with everyone he encountered, up the steps to the front porch, and knocked on the front door. The door opened and standing before him was none other than the woman with the green hair.

She was highly intoxicated as she stumbled toward Officer Thibodaux. He asked for her name, and she answered with a question, "what's your name?"

He answered her question, "I'm Officer Gideon Thibodaux of the Boiling Point Police Department," and asked again, "What's your name?"

The inside of the residence grew quiet as more people began to come toward the door.

Officer Thibodaux stepped away from the threshold of the door, inadvertently inviting the woman out of the residence.

Once she stepped onto the porch, he spun her around and placed her in handcuffs.

The owner of the white Town Car came to the door and asked what was going on.

Officer Thibodaux told him that she was being arrested for weapons charges including aggravated assault for shooting at the store.

The owner assured everyone inside the house that all was well, and Officer Thibodaux left the residence with the woman in custody.

When they returned to the Justice Center, the detention staff began to book her into the jail.

She was clearly too intoxicated to answer any questions and due to the staff being all male, a female jailer was needed to search her person and change her into jail attire.

While waiting for the female jailer, the dispatcher informed Officer Thibodaux that an intoxicated male was in the headquarters' lobby.

By that time, another officer was on-duty and able to speak with the male.

That officer called for Officer Thibodaux to come to the lobby and once he arrived, he saw the man to be none other than the original carrier of the firearm.

The man, also, was highly intoxicated.

He informed Officer Thibodaux that his girlfriend was recently arrested for a crime in which he committed.

Officer Thibodaux asked what crime he was referring to and the man advised "shooting at the store."

Officer Thibodaux escorted the man into the interrogation room and left him there while he briefed his partner.

He explained everything that occurred at the store on Berry Hill Road and what led up to the apprehension of the green haired woman.

Officer Thibodaux explained that the couple was intoxicated, and they needed to keep them separated until they were sober-minded and cleared to be interviewed.

His partner understood and left the headquarters to patrol.

Officer Thibodaux took advantage of the time and began to draft his report from the information he knew.

Late the next afternoon, Officer Thibodaux entered the Justice Center and interviewed the woman. Her name was Hilary Berry. After signing a waiver of her rights, she told him everything that happened at the store.

Interviewer Notes:

They ran out of beer at the party, so they went to get more. Once at the store, they decided to get snacks as well but got too much so her boyfriend had to help carry some.

He wanted to keep his right hand free because he needed to keep his pants from falling due to the weight of the gun.

With his hands full he was not able to support control of the gun, and it slid down his pant leg. He tried to swing it to the other side of his pant leg to keep it from falling out, but his gestures helped it fall to the cuff. Then gravity pulled it out of his pant leg.

She said that she knew the gun was falling so she walked close behind him and as soon as she heard it hit the floor, she knew to grab it. However, with the number of items she had in her hands, it was difficult to put the gun in her waistband and drew the attention of the cashiers.

Hilary said she figured the women saw the gun and became scared because she was drunk but when they began hounding her about stealing merchandise, she grew increasingly mad. She stated she tried to pull the gun out to scare them, but it was caught inside her shirt, then her sister and boyfriend dragged her out of the store.

When they got into the car, she gave her boyfriend the gun and they made out. She told him to "shoot those bitches." and he leaned out the back passenger side window, firing three shots at the store hitting the diesel fuel tanks and the building.

She said the driver did not know they had the gun or that they were going to shoot at the building.

Next, Officer Thibodaux interviewed the man, after receiving a signed waiver of his rights. His name was Gary Addams. Gary's statement was identical to Hilary's.

Interviewer Notes:

Gary said he did not want to take the gun with him to the store but because he did not know anyone at the house where they were partying, he felt more comfortable keeping the gun on his person.

He said that he forgot he had the gun in his waistband until they were already out of the car, and he felt it shift. While they were in the store, the girls were grabbing so much stuff and he told them to stop but they would laugh at him.

He said he knew if he let go of his waistband the gun would fall so, he tied the strings of his sweatpants as tight as he could hoping that the tension would hold the gun in place. It did not work.

Gary said before the gun fell out of his pant leg, he told Hilary that as soon as it dropped to pick it up, and she did.

Before they could set everything down on the counter, the cashier began yelling at Hilary and when Hilary got drunk, she was ready to fight.

He said they knew they needed to get her out of the store as fast as possible. And they could see she was struggling to get the gun out of her waistband.

Gary said once they were in the car, Hilary began making out with him and rubbing her hands across his penis.

He said she was so excited and turned on. She was turning him on, and he wanted to have sex with her in the back seat of the Lincoln.

She leaned into him and whispered into his ear "it would be really hot if you shot those bitches." Then she handed him the gun and sat back.

He leaned over her and kissed her then licked her neck and leaned out the window as the car drove out of the parking lot.

He fired three rounds toward the building not knowing where they would strike.

Officer Thibodaux received the statements from both Gary and Hilary.

They were formally booked into Boiling Point Criminal Justice Center for their individual crimes.

CHAPTER 9

HE'S SPYING ON ME

Officer Thibodaux was back at his desk in headquarters.

All the excitement of the drunken gunslingers caused him to forget about what was waiting under his desk.

And just like before, he found it when he bent down to roll his pant leg down over his boot.

Officer Thibodaux grunted "ugh!" He took out his phone and captured a picture of the object, sending a text to Deputy Chief Perry and Tabitha with the caption:

'HE'S SPYING ON ME!'

The hour was late, and he did not expect a response from either of them, so he was shocked to feel his phone vibrating in the left breast pocket of his uniform shirt.

He removed his phone and looked at the screen. 'Why is he awake at this hour?' thought Officer Thibodaux.

He stood up from his desk as he answered the phone.

"Hello?"

"Is that what I think it is?" asked Deputy Chief Perry.

Sarcastically, Officer Thibodaux responded, "depends on what you think it is."

"Gideon!" chimed Deputy Chief Perry.

Officer Thibodaux laid his body-worn camera on a table near the back door as he walked out and calmed Deputy Chief Perry down.

"I had to buy some time until I was out of the building and put my camera up. I didn't expect you to call so soon." he clarified.

"Yeah, I just happened to be on the toilet when you sent the picture." explained Deputy Chief Perry. "Is that a camera?" he asked. "Where is it?"

Officer Thibodaux began "it's under my desk, directed toward me. I have no idea how long it has been there."

"How'd you find it?" asked Deputy Chief Perry.

"Well, I saw it earlier at the beginning of my shift. That's why I called you. But I got that call and spent all night on it. Made two arrests and paperwork and all. You know. I just happened to sit down at my desk and bent down to fix my pant leg when I saw it again. I decided to send it now before I forget again." noted Officer Thibodaux.

Deputy Chief Perry assured him "okay, Gideon. Stay out of the office for the rest of the night if you can. I'll see you in the morning. Meet me in my office when I get there."

They hung up and Officer Thibodaux went back into the headquarters to shut down his computer and get his camera. He then spent the remainder of his shift patrolling and talking to the women at the Pilot Travel Center.

The next morning, Officer Thibodaux waited for Deputy Chief Perry in the employee parking lot. He was barely awake when Deputy Chief Perry knocked on his window. "Sleeping on the job?" he asked.

"My shift is technically over." answered Officer Thibodaux.

They walked inside the headquarters together and Officer Thibodaux clocked out.

While Officer Thibodaux was not looking, Deputy Chief Perry climbed under his desk and ripped the camera from its base.

"This is bullshit!" he exclaimed.

"This is a wireless camera. He has been watching from his phone. You don't know how long it was under there?" He asked as he turned off the camera and removed the memory card.

"No idea." Officer Thibodaux sighed in disbelief. "What are you going to do with it?" he asked.

"I'm not sure yet. But I am for sure getting it out of here. Come on, let's go to my office. I've got something to show you."

They walked toward Deputy Chief Perry's office, and he reached to unlock the door.

"Ooh! This son of a bitch!" Deputy Chief Perry mumbled through his gritted teeth.

"What's wrong?" asked Officer Thibodaux.

Deputy Chief Perry responded, "This arrogant asshole has been in my office and didn't even bother to lock the door back." 'I wonder if he found my camera,' he thought aloud.

Officer Thibodaux stood behind Deputy Chief Perry and watched him rack his brain on what to do next.

He could see his ears turning red in anger.

Trying to calm him down, Officer Thibodaux suggested "let's go check your camera." He honestly had no idea Deputy Chief Perry had a camera.

"Ye... Yeah. Let's check it before I do something I will not regret." said Deputy Chief Perry.

He came in to support his friend and subordinate against a menacing and hostile chief of police. However, the chief was targeting him also.

Now this was personal and once he checked his camera, he would have the proof.

"Close the door." Deputy Chief Perry told Officer Thibodaux. "Before we check the camera, let's search the office for bugs."

Deputy Chief Perry knew someone had been in his office because the door was left unlocked, something he never does even if he is in a hurry.

He arrived at work later than Officer Thibodaux expected because he stopped at the King's Parish Mall to pick up a hidden camera detector.

"Here, I got two of these. You check over there. Oh, and hey. My camera is under the table next to my desk." Deputy Chief Perry told Officer Thibodaux.

They each took a detector and scanned the office. Together they found two cameras and one wireless surveillance mic.

One camera was a pen camera camouflaged in a cup of pens. The second camera was placed in the top right corner of the window entering Deputy Chief Perry's office. It had a full view of his office. The wireless surveillance mic was taped to the bottom of Deputy Chief Perry's desk.

Deputy Chief Perry was fuming with hatred for Chief Anderson, but he still needed to prove it was him that placed the items in his office.

He went to the table next to his desk hoping they did not find his camera, since they placed their own cameras all over his office.

Deputy Chief Perry reached under the table. Officer Thibodaux watched in uncertainty, his brow growing increasingly hot with curiosity.

Then Deputy Chief Perry stood up saying "there it is."

Officer Thibodaux did not realize he had been holding his breath. He sighed in relief and a bead of sweat rolled downward between his eyes.

"Now, let's check it." said Deputy Chief Perry still unsure if the chief had switched the memory card.

He plugged the card into his computer and waited for it to load. After a few clicks of the mouse, he saw that the memory card was full. Clicking on the third to last clip, they were angered to see who entered the deputy chief's office.

CHAPTER 10

THE PLAN

A few days later Charles called Officer Thibodaux back to his house. He saw the videos Deputy Chief Perry had along with the surveillance equipment that was left in his office and the camera under Officer Thibodaux's desk.

Little did they know, Charles had friends in high places.

When Officer Thibodaux arrived, he was greeted by Tabitha at the front door. "Good evening, Gideon. Can I get you anything to drink?"

"Mike's?" Officer Thibodaux asked.

Tabitha smiled and nodded as they walked through the foyer.

Deputy Chief Perry and Charles were sitting in the living room with another man.

"Ah, Gideon!" Charles said as he stood with his left arm extended. "Come in. Let me introduce you to Brendan Landry."

"Hello Mr. Landry." greeted Officer Thibodaux.

Charles continued, "yes Brendan, here, is an investigator with the Attorney General's Office. Will brought me the items you all found in the headquarters. I downloaded the videos and took pictures of the items then sent them to him asking what we could do. He produced a great plan that's even backed by the Attorney General himself."

Officer Thibodaux looked at Brendan in amazement. "Wow. So, what's the plan?" he asked.

At this time, Tabitha handed him his drink and sat down next to Charles. Officer Thibodaux sat down in the chair next to Deputy Chief Perry.

Brendan began to talk. "Well, Gideon? It is clear to me that you two have provided Tabitha with a list of possible corrupt police officers that includes the chief and commissioner."

He continued, "the Attorney General wants to expose them and any illegal activity in which they are involved. Then he will file charges on them all collectively. This will require more work on your behalf; however, I will personally be there with you."

Deputy Chief Perry and Officer Thibodaux looked puzzled and Deputy Chief Perry asked, "what do you mean you will be there with us? How will you get in? The chief is not willingly going to let an investigator from the A.G.'s office come in."

Brendan laughed and said "who says I need his permission? I will walk into his office tomorrow and tell him I have an investigation in town. That's all he needs to know."

Officer Thibodaux then spoke up and said "that ought to be good. I wish I could see his face when you tell him that. He won't like it. He's a control freak and very paranoid. He's probably freaking out right now about his surveillance equipment."

Tabitha then asked "so, what was on the video? If you can tell me. I promise not to write about it in the Ledger. I know all of this is confidential."

The four men looked at each other. Charles vouched for his wife.

With a nod from Deputy Chief Perry, Charles began to describe the contents of the video on Deputy Chief Perry's camera.

"Well, you see, we were expecting to see Chief Anderson placing the surveillance equipment in Will's office.

Instead, we saw Captain Dupree, Sergeant LeBlanc, and Officer Jacobs enter the office. Fortunately, Will's camera captures audio as well. So, we heard them saying 'he wants them out of sight but with a good view.'

Then Sergeant LeBlanc and Officer Jacobs start arguing over where the best vantage point would be. Meanwhile, Captain Dupree is placing the surveillance mic under the desk.

Captain Dupree finally stands up and whispers a shout 'HEY!! Stick the camera in the corner of that window, just behind the blinds. Let me see the pen.'

He took the pen, clicked a button, and placed it in the cup. He motioned and they all walked out.

Just when we thought that was the end of it, Sergeant LeBlanc and Officer Jacobs came back in. Sergeant LeBlanc was holding a Chromebook.

He opened it, clicked some keys then moved the pen. He stroked a few more buttons of the keyboard then closed the computer.

They left the office but apparently didn't lock the door behind them."

Charles finished his statement.

Tabitha stared in awe.

She finally asked, "does anyone else have a key to your office, Will?"

Deputy Chief Perry finished the sip of drink he had in his mouth and answered, "only Gideon."

The entire room went still, and everyone looked at Officer Thibodaux who was enjoying his Mike's Hard Iced Tea.

"Mm mm." he said, shaking his head as he swallowed a big gulp. "I've got my key right here. The fuck?"

Everyone started laughing. Everyone, that is, except Officer Thibodaux.

He could not believe they would think he would team up with corrupt, criminal police officers.

CHAPTER 11

INVESTIGATOR LANDRY

Three days after their meeting, Brendan Landry walked into the Watts Headquarters of the Boiling Point Police Department.

He showed his badge and I.D. card to the receptionist and announced, "I need to speak with Chief Anderson, please."

The receptionist looked at his I.D. card and said dismissively, "A.G.'s Office, huh? Let me see if he's in."

She then got up from her seat and walked away from her desk, disappearing around a corner.

Brendan looked around the lobby and the office for any cameras.

He noticed there was an alarming number of security cameras. Too many for the space provided.

However, this could be used to his benefit.

Instead of planting a camera, like he planned in the receptionist's absence, he would have his team of cyber security analysts hack into the police department's surveillance system.

While Brendan was scanning and thinking, the receptionist returned. "Chief Anderson will see you now." she reported.

"Thank you." Brendan replied.

She pushed a button under the desk and the door to his left buzzed open.

Brendan walked through the industrial strength metal door and observed yet another camera on the wall above his head.

'Someone has some serious paranoia.' he thought.

He turned to his right and walked through the short hall to the open door that read "CHIEF ANDERSON" in bold black letters on a gold name plate.

Using the knuckle of his middle finger on his right hand, Brendan tapped two times on the door. "Chief?" he called out.

Chief Anderson did not look up as he pretended to type on his computer. "Yes, come in. Sit. I'll be with you in a moment. Just let me finish this email. And send."

He slams his pointer finger down on the enter button as he looks up at Brendan with a half-cocked smile.

"What can I do for you, Mr....?"

Brendan stands and extends his right hand as he begins to introduce himself. "Brendan Land..."

Seeing that Chief Anderson was not interested in the introduction, Brendan retreated his hand as he finished saying his name, "...dry." he mumbled.

Annoyed, Chief Anderson repeated himself. "Yeah, what can I do for you?"

Brendan informed Chief Anderson of the reason for his visit.

"I'm here today as courtesy on behalf of the Attorney General's Office to inform you of an undercover operation that will be taking place in Boiling Point."

Brendan finally had Chief Anderson's attention. But he was not giving him any further information.

"What undercover operation?!" barked Chief Anderson.

"If there's something going on in my city, my office should have been made aware first!"

Brendan stood up and sarcastically said, "that's not how investigations work. Sorry to inform you.

You need more training and less cameras."

He turned to walk out but Chief Anderson stopped him. "What is that supposed to mean?"

Chief Anderson thought Brendan was referring to the missing cameras from Deputy Chief Perry's office and Officer Thibodaux's desk.

Brendan turned and said "there's an overabundance of cameras just in the lobby of your department.

I have not been beyond the administrative side, and I've counted eleven cameras. That's inside the building. You don't have that many outside."

He recalled, "I saw one on the front; overlooking the public parking lot. One over the front door. And one overlooking the employee parking. Am I missing anything, Chief?"

Chief Anderson stood behind his desk not sure what to say.

Brendan chuckled and said, "if there's nothing else, I'll see myself out."

He turned and walked out the door.

Just when Chief Anderson thought he was in the clear, Brendan poked his head back in the door.

"Oh, Chief!" he exclaimed. Chief Anderson, sitting in his chair, jumped. "Maybe next time, you can give me a tour of your nice facility," he suggested.

Chief Anderson reluctantly nodded in agreement.

CHAPTER 12

THE INFORMANT

Officer Thibodaux had not ever collaborated with a Confidential Informant so when he received a social media message from a social media profile identified as "Diddy Bagger" willing to give him information, he was unsure of how to proceed.

Reluctantly, he asked the man what type of information he had.

Depending on the information, Officer Thibodaux would talk to the District Attorney about employing the man as a "C.I."

For several hours, Officer Thibodaux did not hear from the man.

Then, suddenly, he received a long message from a "**No Name**" social media profile.

In the message, No Name began talking about a burglary that occurred at an abandoned two-story residence located in the King neighborhood within the city limits of Boiling Point.

No Name said he bought some light fixtures and a ceiling fan from a known drug user, identified as Corneilus "Rat" Musgrove, who told him the items were hot; meaning they were stolen.

He said Rat and his brother, Andrew "Mole", kicked in the back door of the two-story house and stole the items.

Officer Thibodaux knew what house No Name was referring to because he responded to this burglary as a back-up unit.

Intrigued, he continued reading.

No Name said he took the items to woman's house to try and sell but she could tell they were stolen by the look of them, the condition they were in.

She refused to buy them but told him where he might have luck selling them.

She drove him to a thrift store in the Watts neighborhood owned by Beaux Kipling and his wife, Jennifer.

He said he took the items inside and showed Jennifer, but she was not interested, however Beaux wanted the ceiling fan, so he sold it.

No Name said Beaux and Jennifer sell a lot of stolen items inside their thrift store. He said he could point out some and tell Officer Thibodaux from where the items were stolen and by whom.

Officer Thibodaux thought the information given by this unknown individual, although good, was not enough to take to the District Attorney to put him on an active C.I. payroll.

At best, he would simply be someone providing crime tips to the police department, and he conveyed that to No Name, thanking him for the information.

Two days later, Officer Thibodaux received another message from the profile identified as "Diddy Bagger."

In this message, Bagger said a man named Sam had a large shipment of drugs being brought in from out of town.

He did not say which town, when or how the drugs were being brought in.

The next day, a similar message. Bagger texted "Hot Water, LA. Large Quantity. Watts or Gray. Next few days."

Feeling like this was information he could use; Officer Thibodaux made an appointment with the District Attorney and sent the time to Diddy Bagger.

A few days later, Officer Thibodaux arrived at the District Attorney's office where he met a short red headed Irish man whom he had never seen before.

Officer Thibodaux was off-duty and not in uniform.

Most people would say they could not recognize him out of uniform, but this man acted like he had known Officer Thibodaux his entire life.

He walked a few steps behind Officer Thibodaux with his head down as they climbed the steps of the King County Courthouse and made their way to the District Attorney's office.

Once inside, the man introduced himself as Diddy Bagger.

He told them he had been through this before in another state, and they can check his record.

He said he had been to prison, serving 23 years for arson and attempted murder. He said he was clean now, but he had to leave his home state and ended up there.

He did not expect Boiling Point to be what it was, and he told them they have a huge problem to which he offered his help.

The District Attorney asked for his identifiers to complete a background check and Bagger complied; but asked that he remain anonymous.

He was assured that his information would not be released in any reports and that he would be given a Confidential Informant number that he would go by.

Bagger gave his full name and date of birth and provided the District Attorney with a Georgia photo identification card.

Officer Thibodaux ran a warrant check using the information provided and learned that there was an active warrant for the individual out of Georgia, however it was an in-state pick up only, and they would not place a hold.

Officer Thibodaux returned and relayed the information to the District Attorney who, then, agreed to use Bagger as a C.I. provided the information, he gave was worthwhile.

Bagger proceeded to tell them about the local Irish Mob chapter in Boiling Point.

He told them a man named Antonio was the head of the organization, but he did not live in the city limits.

He said Antonio was on his way to Hot Water to receive a large shipment of meth and that he would be traveling through the Gray neighborhood in a black Dodge pickup.

He told them the supply would go to one of two dealers; a man named Sam, or a man named George.

He had never met them and knew nothing of them, so it was best to get to the load when it arrived in town.

CHAPTER 13

THE BUST STOPS HERE

Being the chief, Marcus Anderson thought he could get away with anything. He had no accountability and no one to hold him accountable.

He had surrounded himself with simpleminded people who only wanted to gain the world at the expense of everyone in it.

Chief Anderson was prepared to use these individuals to get what he wanted and likewise, they were prepared to use him.

Officers patrolling the night shift in the Gray neighborhood saw a Dodge Ram 1500, spray painted with black primer, driving erratically on the eastside of the neighborhood.

The pickup would speed up one residential street then slowly creep through another.

The actions of the vehicle gained the attention of Officer Bucannon.

Officer Bucannon radioed to Officer Morgan about the suspicious behavior and continued following the vehicle at a safe distance.

The vehicle made an abrupt stop from forty-five miles per hour in the center of an intersection.

Officer Bucannon, who was traveling behind the vehicle at forty-three miles per hour, completed an evasive maneuver by tapping his brakes twice, turning his steering wheel to the left to avoid colliding with the pickup, swerving around the truck then turning his steering wheel to the right, before fully applying the brakes and coming to a complete stop directly in front of the Dodge pickup.

The pickup conducted an illegal U-turn in the intersection where it was posted "**NO U-TURN**".

Officer Bucannon pulled to the right side of the road, activated his emergency lights, looked both ways, then turned around and began to pursue the Dodge pickup.

Officer Bucannon alerted Officer Morgan via radio that he was attempting to catch up to the vehicle and the direction of travel.

He then activated his siren and notified the dispatcher that he was in pursuit of the vehicle and gave the description, including the tag which was from out of state.

Officer Morgan arrived at an intersection of Marshall and State Street in the direction the vehicle was traveling.

He exited his patrol unit and removed a case of stop sticks from the trunk. He eagerly waited.

Officer Bucannon advised Officer Morgan over the radio "We're coming up on State Street!"

Officer Morgan did not hesitate. He instantly threw out the stop sticks without a care as to whose vehicle hit them.

The black Dodge drove over them.

Officer Bucannon slowed down.

Officer Morgan ripped the sticks out of the road.

Only the front tires were struck. With a thunderous boom, both front tires exploded.

Air pressure became visible.

Shards of tire rubber were thrown into the dimly lit night sky as the pickup barreled through the Gray neighborhood, the driver beginning to lose control.

As sparks flew from the rims of the front wheels, the Dodge pickup raced through the residential area of the Gray neighborhood toward the business district.

Fortunately, all businesses were closed at this late hour and not many people were on the streets.

Even the bars were shutting down, however there were still a few homeless people and prowlers moving about.

There was one obstacle that stood in the way of the truck leaving the residential area of the Gray neighborhood.

The Sante Fe Railway.

In normal circumstances, this would be an easy feat, but with most of the truck's front wheels shredded and the rims grinded away the truck slammed into the rails nearly flipping end over end.

The truck's rear end raised high in the air.

The driver stared down at the tracks below, everything inside the truck crashing toward the engine.

Then, just like that, everything stopped.

The sound of sirens from outside the vehicle slowly trickled through the cab of the truck and into the driver's ears.

He was unconscious for two minutes, face down, partially laying over the steering wheel.

He was bleeding from his nose, mouth, and ears.

He had a concussion and further unknown injuries.

The two officers parked their patrol units a significant distance away, unsure of which way the truck would land.

They requested additional units, supervisors, fire and EMS, a wrecker, and the Sante Fe Railway investigator to shut down the tracks.

Once the officers had the pickup surrounded and eyes on the driver, and the wrecker was on scene, they hooked onto the rear of the truck and lowered it.

The officers all cautiously approached the vehicle, guns drawn yelling "LET ME SEE YOUR HANDS! SHOW ME YOUR HANDS!"

But the driver was still in a daze.

Sergeant Manwell reached through the broken window of the driver's door and unlocked it. Then from the outside he attempted to open the door, however the crash jammed the front fender into the door preventing it from opening.

The driver, coming to, realized what was happening and began to reach into the passenger side floorboard.

Thinking quickly, Officer Morgan called out to the man "HEY!" and when he looked up, Officer Morgan struck him on the side of the head with the butt of his rifle, knocking him out.

This bought them enough time for the firefighters to pry open the doors so the officers could subdue the driver.

A search incident to arrest was conducted on the vehicle which uncovered a black backpack with a combination of methamphetamines, heroin, crack cocaine, and phencyclidine.

The street value for the weight of drugs in the bag was over a million dollars.

The officers had never seen that much drugs.

There was also a Canik 9 mm caliber pistol inside the bag, a Micro-Roni conversion kit with a Glock 22 .40 caliber under the seat, and a Radical Firearms sixteen-inch 223 AR15 rifle behind the seat.

The driver was identified as Antonio Passat of Crisis Bluff, Louisiana.

The truck was registered in Arkansas.

Antonio had a great trip traveling from Hot Water to Boiling Point.

Driving along the bayous, hearing the chirps of the crickets and the croak of the frogs, feeling the humid air blow through the windows of his truck as the tune of 'ZZ Top' rocked from the stereo.

It was all love, peace, and chicken grease until he crossed the bridge entering the City Limits of Boiling Point.

Boiling Point was easy to get lost in depending on what area you are in. The streets run north, south, east, and west.

But some of the roads of Gray run diagonal making an X in the center of that neighborhood, while others shift one way or the other and the name may not change with the proper shift as they do in Watts.

These unknown geography facts are what posed a problem for Antonio.

Before he knew it, the police were tailing him.

CHAPTER 14

THE DROP

Antonio was transported to Saint Michael Cathedral Hospital in the Watts neighborhood for immediate surgery.

He had swelling on his brain from blunt force trauma to the frontal lobe.

Antonio also had internal bleeding in his torso from broken ribs received during the impact and other injuries.

As soon as Antonio was well enough to speak, Chief Anderson sent Sergeant LeBlanc from the Watts precinct and Sergeant Manwell from the Gray precinct to speak with him.

He wanted to know why Antonio was in his city with that much drugs. To whom was he delivering? And how much was he getting paid for them?

Though, there was one problem.

Antonio was not talking.

Chief Anderson had a solution for people like Antonio.

Lieutenant Menendez.

Lieutenant Menendez just had a way about making unwilling people want to do whatever it was he wanted.

The thing is, he was not even a big guy. He just had a presence that made you want to be obedient... for your safety.

Lieutenant Menendez visited Antonio in the hospital and found out that he was supposed to deliver the load of drugs to 13 Beaumont Circle, Lot 4 to a man named George Groves.

The officers completed the transaction with an undercover officer.

They thought George had the money.

He was upset that "Antonio" was days, not hours, but **DAYS** late. They did not have communication in case he was stopped. The drugs could not be traced to George.

When 'Antonio' finally arrived, George knew something was off because the real Antonio knew George did not have the money.

George's house was not the drop point. George was the contact.

But this person pretending to be Antonio did not know that. He thought he would hand George the bag of drugs and George would hand him a bag of money.

Then all the "cops" would rush in and make the bust. Except, that is not how it worked.

George told this 'Antonio' to get back into his truck, a black Dodge pickup except this pickup was not spray painted with black primer.

Not even matte black.

This truck was shiny, like it was new off the showroom floor.

George was going to find out who this imposter was, so he told him to drive north, out of the Watts neighborhood, toward Lake Charleston in the Cook neighborhood.

Feeling that something was off, the officers tailing them conducted a traffic stop.

They knew they did not have a lawful reason for the traffic stop other than the undercover officer's safety, so they made something up.

Sergeant LeBlanc pulled 'Antonio' from the vehicle to "issue a citation" for improper tag display.

When 'Antonio' returned to the pickup, Sergeant LeBlanc approached and asked "one more thing before you leave. Is there anything illegal inside the vehicle?"

'Antonio' chuckled. "Illegal?" he asked.

"Yeah, you know. Guns, drugs, grenades, substantial amounts of cash, dead bodies. You know, anything illegal or suspicious?" Sergeant LeBlanc asked.

'Antonio' looked at George then back at Sergeant LeBlanc. "Naw. I don't believe so. Why do you ask?"

Sergeant LeBlanc grew a suspicious look on his face. "Why did you look at him?" he asked 'Antonio'.

"Huh? Whu... I mean that's just a strange question is all. Ain't nobody ever asked me that before. Took me by surprise." 'Antonio' announced.

George sat quietly in the passenger seat watching the spectacle these officers were putting on.

"Well, you won't mind if I search the vehicle, would you?" asked Sergeant LeBlanc.

Again, 'Antonio' looked at George then back at Sergeant LeBlanc.

"I tell you what, my friend here is in a great big hurry to get where he's going and when I drop him off, I'd love to oblige you." 'Antonio' suggested.

George was humored and annoyed by this tirade from both 'Antonio' and Sergeant LeBlanc.

George had sold drugs for long enough that he knew when someone was setting him up. But this time he did not know what was in the bag, so he just played it cool.

It was only a couple of grams, and they could not hold him for it.

He knew what was supposed to be in it, but there was no way they would bring that much and lose it all.

George decided to put a stop to the charades and told the officers "it's okay. I'm in no hurry."

Besides, he knew the truck was not his, the bag was not his, and most importantly the drugs were not his. They could not prove otherwise.

As soon as they exited the vehicle more patrol units arrived, and Sergeant LeBlanc opened the passenger side door and went straight for the bag.

He pulled the backpack out, placed it on the tailgate and opened it.

"Ah! What's this?" Sergeant LeBlanc said, looking at George. "Looks like you should have kept your mouth shut."

"Wait, wait, wait, wait." George stuttered. "That's not mine. I've never seen that bag." he pleaded. "This guy just picked me up!"

Knowing exactly how much trouble he was in, George tried to run, but they tackled him and several of the officers began hitting and kicking him.

One officer broke through the crowd and came to George's aid. He did not care what type of person George was, he did not deserve the treatment he was receiving.

From that day on Officer Thibodaux had a mark on his back.

George was treated for his injuries and given a new task.

He was going to work for Chief Anderson now under the ruse of a confidential informant.

However, instead of returning information of drug deals, he would return money from the drug deals to Sergeant LeBlanc and if he missed a payment, he would receive a visit from Lieutenant Menendez.

George missed a few payments here and there. Some because the load was not as much as expected and others because he simply did not want to pay.

He had to hide out for a few days, away from home, but Lieutenant Menendez always managed to find him.

CHAPTER 15

PRAYER WORKS

Officer Thibodaux was enjoying his last day off when a notification screeches from his department issued cell phone — The display reads "Dispatch to all available units!! There has been a report of a Signal 30 **OFFICER DOWN** at 13 Beaumont Circle; Lot 4. Barricaded Subject. **ALL AVAILABLE UNITS REQUESTED!!**"

Officer Thibodaux was on the swat team's Critical Response Unit as a negotiator.

He and his team set up their command post near the suspect's house. Officer Thibodaux did not know it at the time, but this house belonged to an old friend. One he had not seen in a few weeks.

The last time Officer Thibodaux saw this friend was during another traumatic episode, in which he attempted suicide.

This time he had killed a police officer.

Not just any police officer, this was a friend of Chief Anderson.

Lieutenant Menendez had gone to 13 Beaumont Circle; Lot 4 with specific instructions from Chief Anderson to ruff up the homeowner, George Groves.

George owed money for drugs and threatened to rat out the corrupt officers because he would not pay them.

When he saw Lieutenant Menendez stop in front of his house, he went to his safe and grabbed his deceased father's 12-gauge shotgun.

Loading the gun with a slug shell, George took aim and fired the round at Lieutenant Menendez's midsection striking him below his protective body armor and ripping through his liver.

Lieutenant Menendez stumbled backwards and collapsed in the front yard.

Neighbors heard the gunshot and saw the officer go down. They called 911.

The first responding officer attempted to retrieve Lieutenant Menendez, however, George opened fire on him, shooting Lieutenant Menendez's lifeless body.

The responding officer radioed for backup and described the scene.

Tabitha arrived at the scene near the Incident Command Post where all the top brass was stationed.

She and two of her employees began recording audio and video as well as taking pictures of the scene.

Tabitha overheard Chief Anderson yelling inside a tent and went to peek inside it.

Chief Anderson was yelling to the swat commander, saying "I want this piece of shit dead. Do you hear me? Kill him. Do NOT let Thibodumbass and those other idiots talk him out. Kill his ass like he killed my officer."

Tabitha recorded the tyrant's outburst on video and painted it all over social media.

Another negotiator who follows Tabitha's V feed received a notification with the caption:

'TYRANT CHIEF ORDERS EXECUTION.'

He nudged Officer Thibodaux and showed him the post and they watched it.

Officer Thibodaux then left the command post in a hurry to find the swat commander.

Officer Thibodaux ran up to the swat commander and ordered him to stand down.

The swat commander dismissed him saying "pfft. I have direct orders from the chief himself to take this guy out. Get out of my face, Thibodaux."

Officer Thibodaux held up his phone with the headline and said “I know. Now stand down.”

The swat commander looked at the phone in disbelief and ordered his team to stand down. He asked Officer Thibodaux “So what's your play here?”

Officer Thibodaux was unsure because he had not received enough information of the occupant inside the house. “I don’t know yet. I need to try to talk to this guy. Find out who he is and how to get him out. But I need to know your guys won’t kill him when he comes out.”

The swat commander glared at him. “If he comes out.”

Officer Thibodaux assured him, “he’ll come out.”

The swat commander sneered “dead or alive, I guess.”

Officer Thibodaux returned to his command post.

He was not sure who all he could trust, on his own team even, so he kept his thoughts to himself.

Deputy Chief Perry arrived and went directly to the C.R.U. command post. “Please tell me you guys have this shit under control!” he roared.

Officer Thibodaux informed him they had it managed for now. He asked “William, can you make sure the Chief doesn’t interfere? Let us work.”

Deputy Chief Perry nodded. "I got you, Gideon."

Then he left the command post.

Officer Thibodaux and Officer Burrow began their attempts to contact George inside his house.

They tapped into his landline phone, but it was disconnected. They tapped into his cell phone, but it was not accepting phone calls.

Finally, Officer Thibodaux read the full name of the suspect and realized he knew him.

He used his P.A. speaker to call out to George.

"GEORGE GROVES!" He called over the loudspeaker. **"MY NAME IS GIDEON THIBODAUX. I'M AN OFFICER WITH THE BOILING POINT POLICE DEPARTMENT. I WANT TO TALK WITH YOU. JUST YOU AND I FOR ONLY A MOMENT TO SORT THIS OUT. CAN I SAFELY COME IN?"**

There was no movement inside the house for several minutes.

Officer Thibodaux continued **"COME ON, GEORGE! YOU KNOW ME. NO ONE ELSE WILL COME INSIDE UNLESS YOU SAY IT'S OKAY."**

Just then the front door opened displaying the pitch-black interior of the residence.

George did not say anything; however, Officer Thibodaux took this as an invitation to come in.

His colleagues thought this was suicide, but Officer Thibodaux pleaded the Blood of Jesus over himself as he stepped forward, walking passed the deceased body of Lieutenant Menendez.

As soon as he entered the house, the front door slammed shut.

"Why did you come in here, Gideon?" George asked. "You know I could kill you like I killed that crooked cop."

"I know you could." Officer Thibodaux responded. "But I want you to get out of this alive. That's why I came in here. A lot of those cops out there DO want you dead. I will not lie. But I'll do everything in my power to see to it that you live."

George scoffed and shook his head. "Live? No way I'll live. They'll kill me as soon as I step out the door."

"Can I show you something?" Officer Thibodaux asked. He removed his phone from his breast pocket and turned on the screen revealing the video Tabitha published.

George became livid. "See! That's exactly what I mean. They're not going to let me walk out of here. You should just go now before I am forced to kill you too, Gideon."

But Officer Thibodaux stood his ground.

"No, George. You're not listening to me. This has been published. Everyone can see what type of person he is now. And I don't know what caused you to kill Lieutenant Menendez, but I have my own suspicions.

They WILL NOT shoot you because of this video. There are cameras all over your street out there. They won't take that shot."

George still was not convinced that his life was safe in Officer Thibodaux's hands.

He decided that if he was going to die today, he needed to tell Officer Thibodaux why he killed Lieutenant Menendez.

"Listen, Gideon. I've been on drugs for a long time. Meth, heroin, crack. Hell, I've even developed an embalming fluid capsule with MDMA inside it. Shit's good.

These cops stopped me one night and found a shit load of dope on me. They beat the living fuck out of me and took my load. They asked who I was selling it for, and I told them I made it myself and that I had a buyer who was paying one million dollars for this load.

That's when they knew they had me.

They let me go with the load and I made the delivery. Then they stopped me a few blocks from my house and took my money. They left me with five hundred dollars and told me that was plenty.

They then told me every time I made a delivery they wanted to know, and they would keep the 'good' cops off me.

This was working for several weeks until I found out a few days ago that they were doing the same thing to my customer and taking a percentage of the drugs. That's when I started dodging them. I stopped coming home after the drops.

They caught on and broke in a few times beating me up and stealing my money, threatening that the next time it would be my life.

When I saw Lieutenant Menendez, I thought it was over for me, so I decided to stop him before he killed me."

Officer Thibodaux, again, assured George that he would be safe leaving the house. He also showed him that he recorded his testimony and that it could be used to take down the corrupt officers.

He asked George if he was ready to go out. George was not sure.

Officer Thibodaux offered to pray with George if it would calm his nerves.

George agreed.

Officer Thibodaux, facing George, placed his hands on George's shoulders, bowed his head and closed his eyes.

He began praying:

"Our Father, which art in heaven, hallowed be thy name. Thy kingdom come; thy will be done on earth as it is in heaven. Give us this day our daily bread and forgive us our trespasses, as we forgive those who trespass against us. Lead us not into temptation but deliver us from evil. For thine is the kingdom, the power, and the glory, for ever and ever.
Amen."

George stared at him for the first half of the prayer not sure if this was a trick but once he saw the sincerity in Officer Thibodaux's face, he relaxed and closed his eyes.

"Amen." George declared as Officer Thibodaux closed the prayer.

He felt at ease because he trusted Officer Thibodaux.

With his hands on George's shoulders, Officer Thibodaux looked into his eyes and asked, "are you ready?"

George looked back at him and seriously asked in a joking manner "would you be, if you were me?"

Officer Thibodaux removed his handcuffs, gave George a friendly hug, then cuffed him behind his back.

They both took one last deep breath before Officer Thibodaux opened the front door and together, they walked out of the house.

The crowd outside the house erupted.

Some cheered and praised "**GREAT JOB!**" and "**THANK YOU FOR PROTECTING OUR COMMUNITY!**"

Others were angry, including the police officers that surrounded him "**PIECE OF SHIT COP KILLER SHOULD HAVE HIS BRAINS BLOWN OUT!**"

Officer Thibodaux walked swiftly with George to his patrol car and drove him directly to the Boiling Point Justice Center where he was booked in for the charges of:

"FIRST DEGREE MURDER" And "AGGRAVATED ASSAULT AND BATTERY WITH A DEADLY WEAPON."

CHAPTER 16

HEADS WILL ROLL

Chief Anderson was highly pissed off by what happened at the Groves' incident. Not only did he lose what *he* considered a "good officer," he lost a close friend, and he wanted to honor his memory.

Chief Anderson ordered an extremely obtuse plaque with Lieutenant Menendez's name and badge number engraved in it along with the words:

"A HERO. A WARRIOR. A FRIEND."

He hung the plaque in the lobby of the Watts Headquarters.

Chief Anderson vowed to get revenge on Officer Thibodaux and George for his friend's death. This was Officer Thibodaux's last straw.

He gathered all his fellow corrupt supervisors and officers, and they decided to murder Officer Thibodaux.

They needed it to look like an offender did it. Someone who held a grudge against him.

But the people who hated Officer Thibodaux most, were his own co-workers.

Chief Anderson began putting his plan into motion. He utilized officers from every precinct.

He let his anger and hunt for revenge guide him. He was arrogant and a narcissist. However, he was quickly spiraling out of control.

Meanwhile Brendan was working behind the scenes also.

He asked a few officers from the King, Cook, and Gray precincts to work undercover for the Attorney General's Office.

He assured them they would be compensated for their help should they gather any information regarding Chief Anderson.

The officers each reached out to their closest precinct partners, asking if they heard about what happened in Watts.

The Cook precinct was too far away, and they rarely visited Watts, however the Gray precinct had a close working relationship with the Watts precinct and some of their officers trained regularly with Chief Anderson, Captain Dupree, Lieutenant Menendez, Sergeant LeBlanc, and Officer Jacobs.

These were loyal officers. They were the officers that held up George and divided his drugs and money with the Chief and other Watts officers. This would be from where the information would come.

Officer Blake worked nights with Officer Morgan. Officer Morgan trained in Muay Thai and kickboxing with Officer Jacobs for the past 5 years. They decided to become police officers together but were stationed in different precincts.

One night while on break at a convenience store, Officer Blake asked Officer Morgan how he felt about the incident in Watts. Officer Morgan shrugged his shoulders. Not certain of Officer Blake's motives, he asked "why do you ask?"

Officer Blake took a sip of coffee and said "I'm just hearing a lot of mixed things. Some good about this officer and some bad about the lieutenant. I just don't know."

Officer Morgan looked at him with anger and said "you look here. Jose Menendez was a good officer. A good guy and a damn good friend. That lowlife Groves took him away from us for no reason and that piece of shit excuse for a cop, Thibodaux is going to pay. Life for a life."

Officer Blake reared his head back and raised his hands to say 'enough.' He gave Officer Morgan a discerning smile along with a side-eye.

CHAPTER 17

A TIME TO KILL

Officer Thibodaux had learned too much about Chief Anderson's illegal activity.

Although the A.D.A. would not accept his claims and told him it was a City problem and the Commissioner turned the reports back over to the Chief, Officer Thibodaux had stuck his nose in too much of Chief Anderson's business.

And it was time to tie up loose ends.

With Lieutenant Menendez dead, Chief Anderson promoted Sergeant LeBlanc to Lieutenant.

He also promoted Officer Jacobs to Sergeant and moved Officer Morgan from the Gray neighborhood to the Watts neighborhood and promoted him to Sergeant as well.

Chief Anderson told Sergeant Morgan that the switch would take place the next evening at shift change and to meet at the Watts Headquarters.

But first he had one last assignment to complete in the Gray neighborhood.

Sergeant Morgan went to work as scheduled in the Gray neighborhood and patrolled as normal.

Except on this night, he knew he was going to be a part of something major.

This event would turn these officers from mafia-type made men to definite hit men for the largest crime organization in King County and Central Louisiana.

And the person leading the five-man charge to fight this organization would soon come up missing.

Well into the night, Samson Davenport was sleeping in his room.

Samson was a known drug dealer, and, like George, he was one Lieutenant Menendez had to visit often for not delivering his share of supply to the right officer.

Chief Anderson decided it was time to cut Samson out of the loop, except this time it would be done under the cover of night with two sergeants and a third to respond if needed.

Sergeant Manwell and Sergeant Newell left their phones at the Gray headquarters then drove toward Samson's house.

They stopped a few blocks away and blacked out before pulling up to his house.

The sergeants covered their torsos with level IV ballistics (stab + bullet proof) vests and their faces with Kevlar balaclava masks.

They wore gloves with raised knuckles made of metal and quietly approached the steps leading to the front door.

Just like George before him, Samson had become highly paranoid and set up tripwires throughout his house.

These tripwires were not set to explode but instead to alert him that someone was inside the house.

Sergeant Newell used a pick set to unlock the door. As soon as the door opened, it put pressure on one of the wires. A buzzer was set off in Samson's room which slightly roused him.

However, a step on a weak floor joist woke him from his sleep.

Fearing that this was not a dream, Samson grabbed his cellphone and tapped the emergency button at the bottom of the screen.

The line connected. The dispatcher answered "Boiling Point 911. How may I direct your call?"

Samson whispered back "I'm at 2315 Southeast 9th Boulevard in the Gray neighborhood. Someone has broken into my house."

Just then Samson looked up from his hiding spot and saw two dark figures standing in front of him. Suddenly he did not feel this was a simple burglary.

They were here for him.

The two men grabbed Samson, dragging him into the living room where they very violently began a vicious assault on him.

They punched, and kicked his head and torso, striking him with brass knuckles and night sticks, until they heard the voice of the dispatcher on the phone, "Sir, help is on the way!"

The two sergeants knew that Sergeant Morgan was on duty and was supposed to respond if needed.

The only problem was - there were other officers on duty as well and they would have heard that call.

The sergeants quickly ran out of the house and jumped into their car. They were not sure if they beat Samson to death, but it felt good to get some aggression out.

The tires squealed as the car turned in the street driving back the way it came.

Samson crawled to the door and saw that it was a black four door sedan. He told the dispatcher before he passed out.

The responding unit passed a vehicle matching the description and turned around activating its lights and sirens.

The vehicle immediately pulled over.

Unaware of who was inside, the officer cautiously approached with his right hand resting on his gun, fingers wrapped around the handle and the hood of the holster unlocked.

He drew his flashlight and shined it through the rear driver side window as he approached to illuminate the interior of the car.

Then he saw the patch on the sleeve of the passenger and became confused but continued his trek toward the driver's door.

"Good evening. I'm Sergeant Morgan with the Boiling Point Police Department," before he could say anymore Sergeant Manwell interrupted him. "Morgan? You had us going there for a bit. What's up?"

Sergeant Morgan reaches the driver side window and sees the two sergeants riding tandem in an unmarked undercover unit. Making small talk for his camera he says, "I didn't know you two were out tonight."

"Yeah, Cap' had us working on something." Sergeant Newell responded. "Oh yeah. You get it finished?" Officer Morgan asked.

Sergeant Manwell answered, “No. We were interrupted.”

Sergeant Morgan understood and slapped the roof of the car. “Well, I’ll let you guys be on your way.” Then he turned off his camera as he turned away from the car.

Throwing his camera in the passenger seat of his patrol car, the three met in the middle of the street.

“Fucker saw us coming. Was on the phone with dispatch when we arrived.” Sergeant Manwell whispered.

“I’m going to the house in response to that call. My guess is the guy doesn’t know you were cops. So, here’s what we’re going to do.” Sergeant Morgan told the pair.

He then produced an elaborate plan to kill Samson and the three returned to his house.

Sergeant Morgan told dispatch that he was no longer out with the suspicious vehicle and that it was not the vehicle from the burglary.

He went to Samson’s house notifying dispatch again. Hearing a car outside, Samson called 911 and told the operator that he believed the burglars were back.

The dispatcher told him that an officer just checked out at his residence, and they could see him on their GPS locator.

He asked if they would stay on the phone just in case.

Sergeant Morgan knocked on the front door and Samson opened it.

Seeing him in uniform with his supervisor stripes, shiny collar brass, crisp tie with a sparkling tie pin, tying in with his sharp gig line meeting directly in the center of his body three inches below his belly button where the buckle of his leather duty belt shined like freshly cleaned glass.

The crease of his slacks was thick, sharp, and led down to boots so clean Samson could see his reflection.

It was like looking at the T1000 from Terminator 2: Judgment Day.

"Hello sir. I am Sergeant Morgan with the Boiling Point Police Department. You called in reference to a burglary that occurred at this address just a little while ago, is that correct?"

Samson put the phone up to his ear and assured the dispatcher that everything was okay now. The police were here.

After hanging up he responded. "Ye... yes, sir. These two guys. I... I don't even know how they got in. They were like ninjas. They didn't break in. But I locked the door. I always lock the door." he recalled.

"But I set these traps, see." he pointed to the wires behind the door. "These tripwires, they go to buzzers in my room and this." Samson ran to the hallway. "This plank in the floor is weak. And."

Samson began rambling on as he walked through his house showing Sergeant Morgan where the two men found him and where they dragged him to and where they beat him.

But Sergeant Morgan really was not particularly interested. He interrupted Samson, saying "sir, if I were to bring the two guys here, do you think you could identify them?"

Samson knew he could not I.D. the two men.

He did not see their faces. They were wearing masks, it was dark, and the entire time he was trying his best to cover his face with his arms and hands.

"No, sir. I don't think I could." Samson answered.

"Would you try?" Sergeant Morgan asked. "We caught two guys fleeing the area in a black sedan and we want to be sure it was them. The thing is we do not have any evidence except the car. And do you know how many black sedans there are in Boiling Point, Louisiana?"

Hearing that the men in the black sedan were captured, Samson felt at ease. He was prepared to face his demons.

"Sure," he said with confidence. "Whatever it takes to put these guys away."

Sergeant Morgan advised him that he needed to go with him to the Gray headquarters to identify the duo. He said it would be safe. They would be behind a two-way mirror and would not see him.

Samson walked with Sergeant Morgan out to his patrol unit.

He sensed something was off about the car and felt a loom fall over him; but before he reached the passenger side door, he was shot in the head by a 9mm carbine rifle with a silencer on it by Sergeant Manwell, a sniper on the Boiling Point SWAT team.

Sergeant Morgan had covered his door with plastic to prevent any blood splatter from getting on his car and they used that plastic to wrap Samson's body.

They then took his body to an abandoned train station where the police department stored old evidence in a safe.

Captain Dupree and Chief Anderson met them at the train station to unlock the safe.

Then they set motion for phase two of the plan.

CHAPTER 18

SUSPENDED

Brendan set up the appointment with the Attorney General and called Officer Thibodaux to tell him about it. "Meet us at the A.G.'s Office Thursday at seven thirty sharp."

Officer Thibodaux was prepared but nervous. He went in to work and within an hour of being on shift, Captain Dupree called him back to Headquarters over the radio.

'What? Why is he out this late?' Thought Officer Thibodaux. 'He must be up to something no good.'

Officer Thibodaux arrived at Headquarters and saw Sergeant Lablanc's patrol unit in the employee parking lot next to Captain Dupree's. Officer Jacobs and Officer Morgan's personal vehicles were parked in the employee parking lot as well.

'What's going on?' he thought.

Officer Thibodaux called Deputy Chief Perry and Charles telling them something was going on. He told them to stay on the phone but mute their ends.

Tabitha grabbed her voice recorder and began recording.

Phase two of Chief Anderson's plan was to have Captain Dupree bring Officer Thibodaux in after he had already started his shift.

And with a council of his fellow supervisors, Captain Dupree would inform Officer Thibodaux of an ongoing internal investigation in which they believe there was malice, insubordination, threat to public health, and violation of department policy conducted on his behalf; therefore, they were suspending him indefinitely without pay, pending the results of the investigations.

Officer Thibodaux walked into the department.

"Have a seat." Captain Dupree told Officer Thibodaux.

"What's going on?" he asked.

"We'll ask the questions!" shouted Sergeant LeBlanc.

"Have a seat." Captain Dupree said again. This time a little more stern.

Officer Thibodaux looked at the row of chairs then at the officers standing in the corner.

"Nah, I'm good. I think I'll stand." he said.

Sergeant LeBlanc slammed his fist on the table. "Sit your ass down, you insubordinate fucktard!" he shouted.

Captain Dupree raised his hand in front of Sergeant LeBlanc to settle him.

Officer Thibodaux did not move.

Captain Dupree told him, “I need you to sign this disciplinary form, and turn in your badge and gun.

You’ve been suspended pending an investigation into the Groves incident.”

“What? You’ve got to be kidding me? You have no grounds to suspend me. I did nothing wrong at that call.

In fact, I ended it peacefully. Which is my job as a negotiator.

George, Mr. Groves is in jail and Lieutenant Menendez will get justice.”

Just then Officer Morgan stepped forward and shouted “don’t you dare say his name. You have no right to say his goddamn name.

Jose was my friend, and you got him killed. I should drop you where you stand.”

Officer Thibodaux turned toward Officer Morgan with his hand on duty pistol.

By this point, Deputy Chief Perry was in his patrol unit racing to Headquarters trying to put a stop to this onslaught of betrayal to their oath of office and abuse of power by Captain Dupree and Sergeant LeBlanc.

Tabitha video called Brendan who was in a meeting with other investigators from the Attorney General's Office and the Louisiana State Police for a different matter.

They all listened in on the call.

It seemed this was an urgent matter. An officer's life was surely in danger.

Was Officer Thibodaux's paranoid thoughts a valid reality?

"What? Are you going to kill me too?" asked Officer Morgan.

"I didn't kill anyone," Officer Thibodaux declared. "I only saved a life from a bunch of killers and dirty cops."

He ripped his badge off his uniform shirt and threw it at Captain Dupree.

"Contact my lawyer when you decide I can come back, but I ain't signing shit!" he yelled before storming out the door.

Officer Morgan and Officer Jacobs began to chase him but stopped when they saw that Deputy Chief Perry was pulling into the parking lot as Officer Thibodaux climbed down the stairs.

Officer Jacobs looked out the window, "what is he doing here?" he asked concerningly.

"Don't worry about him." Captain Dupree mumbled.

CHAPTER 19

WHERE'S GIDEON

Charles ended the three-way call then called Deputy Chief Perry directly.

"Sounds like you got there just in time." he said in a sarcastic tone.

"Yeah. He isn't doing too well." Deputy Chief Perry responded.

Charles replied, "get him home, let him get cleaned up and you all meet at my place. Tell him to bring a few days' worth of clothes."

Deputy Chief Perry drove Officer Thibodaux straight home and gave him the instructions.

Then he left to go switch from his patrol unit to his personal car. The patrol unit had a tracking device inside it.

Deputy Chief Perry arrived at Charles and Tabitha's house a brief time later and did not see Officer Thibodaux's car outside.

He called his phone, but it just rang several times before going to voicemail. He thought Charles parked the car inside his garage and he was just away from his phone.

Deputy Chief Perry walked to the door and knocked. Tabitha answered and looking around asked "where's Gideon?"

Deputy Chief Perry looked stunned. He said "uh, you mean he isn't here?"

They panicked.

"Charles!" Tabitha yelled. "Gideon! He's missing."

Charles, in a calm manner, asked "what do you mean? Are you sure he is missing? When is the last time anyone has talked to him?"

Deputy Chief Perry replied "I dropped him off at his house. I told him to get some clothes and meet us here. He wanted to drive his own car, and I needed to drop off my patrol unit before I came over. I called his phone when I got here because I didn't see his car outside. No answer."

For the first time since they have been married, Tabitha saw panic in Charles' face.

They all listened to the suspension meeting. They heard how mad Sergeant LeBlanc and Officer Morgan were. Was it possible that they followed Deputy Chief Perry and Officer Thibodaux?

Charles, Tabitha, and Deputy Chief Perry jumped in one of Charles' cars. They rushed to Officer Thibodaux's house.

Deputy Chief Perry called Brendan on the way. "Gideon is missing. Meet us at his house."

Charles' car screeched to a halt in front of Officer Thibodaux's driveway. His front door was wide open.

"Stay here." whispered Deputy Chief Perry.

He drew his pistol and crept toward the door.

What he saw made him cringe. He dropped his head and covered his mouth with the back of hand.

Tears began to flow from his eyes.

Deputy Chief Perry had to enter the house to clear it for any armed assailants, so he quickly dried his eyes, wiping the tears from his cheeks.

He took a deep breath and stepped into the house.

"BPPD!" he shrieked, his voice cracking from being choked up with fear. "Come out with your hands up!"

He continued yelling as he made his way through the house, clearing his throat.

"BPPD! Show yourself. Hands up!"

Deputy Chief Perry cleared the entire house. No one was there. No one, except the body in the living room.

He made his way back to the front door and was met by Charles, Tabitha, Brendan, and the Louisiana State Police Swat team.

Crying, Tabitha asked "is that?"

"I don't know," Deputy Chief Perry answered.

The head was missing from the body.

"We have to wait for the crime scene unit to get here." Deputy Chief Perry said. "They can check the finger-prints."

Everyone walked away from the house and the L.S.P. set up a perimeter throughout the neighborhood.

Some officers from the Boiling Point Police Department arrived to show their respects and offer support. However, there was a noticeable amount missing.

Commissioner Hayes, Chief Anderson, Captain Dupree, Sergeant LeBlanc, Officer Jacobs, and Officer Morgan were not present.

Deputy Chief Perry called Chief Anderson to ask why he was not there. The line rang but he did not answer. Deputy Chief Perry left a message.

He called two more times however neither time did it ring. He knew Chief Anderson was screening his calls because they went directly to voicemail.

The Louisiana State Police C.S.U. arrived on scene and began to process it.

Because an officer was involved, their office would have to process the scene anyway.

There was an ungodly amount of blood all over the house, not just the living room.

It was clear that a struggle took place inside the residence.

There were bullet holes throughout the house. Blood splatter was on the walls and ceilings of the hallway leading to the bedrooms.

Officer Thibodaux lived alone. He was separated from his wife and had not seen his two children in a year and a half.

The crime scene analyst scanned the deceased right pointer finger.

Everyone waited with anticipation.

She came out of the house and called Brendan over, "It's not your guy."

Brendan's head bowed; his shoulders shrunk.

Charles, Tabitha, and Deputy Chief Perry saw the change in Brendan's body language and feared the worst.

Was the body in the living room that of Gideon's?

They still had no answers.

Brendan turned and looked at them. His bottom lip rolled inside his mouth; his top teeth lightly gritting the skin of his bottom lip.

He rubbed his head with his left hand; running his fingers through his hair while he leaned on his right foot with his right hand on his hip, thinking of what to tell the group.

He took in a deep breath and slowly exhaled, then stretched his arms out in front of himself as he walked toward the group with a forced smile saying "Well, guys, I have good news and bad news; which do you want first?"

Brendan nervously chuckled but knowing the seriousness of the matter he continued; "That is not Gideon's body."

Charles, William, and Tabitha all sighed in relief.

"Oh, thank God!" Tabitha breathed out as though she had been holding her breath.

Then the realization set in.

Tabitha's eyes, red and puffy from where she had been crying before, began to swell with tears. Her heart began to race, and her breathing quickened.

She could feel it. She was about to have a full-fledged panic attack.

She quickly turned and sunk her face into Charles' chest to hide her flushed, red cheeks.

Charles embraced his wife, wrapping his strong arms around her long torso ensuring her with his presence that she was safe.

In that moment, Charles did not see Tabitha as his brave, independent investigative reporting wife; he saw her as the scared, timid journalist who had a panic attack before interviews at the beginning of her career.

He calmed Tabitha by reminding her to say what she can feel - his soft cotton LSU polo shirt, smell – the Tom Ford Tobacco Vanille Eau De Parfum fragrance he often wore, and see – Charles' smooth jawline, his green eyes, and fiery red hair. Tabitha was finally at ease.

However, that peace would be disrupted when William spoke up. “Whose body is it? And what about Gideon?”

Brendan spoke honestly, "We don't know. They are taking swabs of blood, hair follicles, his toothbrush, and fingerprints throughout his house for comparison."

He looked at Tabitha, "Don't worry, we will catch whoever is responsible for this."

William felt invisible but it was his friend that was missing; and he felt responsible.

"How can you all just stand here? I know who did this. Look around you. Who is not here? That tells me everything I need to know." William angrily shouted.

Brendan, Charles, and Tabitha knew William was referring to Chief Anderson and his crew of corrupt misfit supervisors.

However as for the L.S.P., who were actively working a murder crime scene, they had only one suspect and one question.

Where was Gideon?

CHAPTER 20

MUTINY

Mr. Benoit, when Officer Thibodaux was suspended on March 24th, 2021, I was on the phone with my end muted.

He returned to the Police Department at the demand of Sergeant LeBlanc via radio.

Officer Thibodaux arrived at the Police Department at 1908 hours and entered the Patrol Room where Captain Dupree and Sergeant LeBlanc met him.

Captain Dupree told Officer Thibodaux to sit down but Officer Thibodaux asked why.

I could hear the nervousness and anger in his voice as he answered shakily.

Sergeant LeBlanc yelled at Officer Thibodaux about questioning their authority.

Captain Dupree lowered his voice and told Officer Thibodaux to sit down again but this time he refused, saying he would rather stand, indicating a lack of trust.

Sergeant LeBlanc shouted at him to sit down. A thud sound echoed in the receiver of the phone,

as though he pounded on the table with his fist or palm and Sergeant LeBlanc called Officer Thibodaux outside of name.

Officer Thibodaux, his voice still shaking, spoke softly and through gritted teeth told him no.

Captain Dupree continued talking by explaining to Officer Thibodaux that he was being placed on suspension, pending an investigation into his conduct during the Groves incident.

He provided Officer Thibodaux with a copy of the Department Notice of Discipline form and informed him that there were complaints against him from the SWAT team commander and his team although he did not present those complaints.

Sergeant LeBlanc began to explain the reprimand and interview Officer Thibodaux. He told Officer Thibodaux to sign the reprimand form.

Officer Thibodaux asked who was conducting the investigation and Sergeant LeBlanc advised that he was the lead investigator.

Officer Thibodaux requested a separate set of supervisors, unbiased to himself, conduct the investigation because he had filed complaints against the two in front of him.

I was not aware, at the time, of the other officers in the room until Sergeant Morgan spoke out.

Officer Thibodaux and Sergeant Morgan got into a heated exchange because Officer Thibodaux said Lieutenant Menendez's name.

Officer Thibodaux was not required to speak to them without his attorney or FOP rep. He was not advised of his rights as a citizen nor was he informed of his willingness to cooperate as an officer.

Officer Thibodaux was demanded to acknowledge and sign the reprimand forms whether he agreed to them or not, which he did not and would not sign.

Officer Thibodaux was reprimanded and suspended without cause, providing there were no evidence to support such claims of: 1. Malice; 2. Insubordination; 3. Threat to Public Health; and 4. Violation of Department Policy.

Officer Thibodaux turned over his department issued equipment identified as:

- ONE BLACK POLYMER/STEEL Glock 17 9mm pistol with one Department issued Glock 17 9mm magazine.

- Duty belt consisting of -- one Taser with holster AND UNSPENT CARTRIDGE, one flashlight-mounted Safariland Glock 17 holster, two handcuff pouches with handcuff (personally purchased handcuffs), personally purchased magazine holder with two Department issued Glock 17 9mm magazines, radio holder and radio, flashlight with holder and key holder with Department and unit keys.
- Department issued uniform including: outer vest carrier with Department issued vest, Department badge, Department Polo shirt, and Department issued jacket.

I helped Officer Thibodaux remove some personal items from his patrol unit and drove him home.

Officer Thibodaux was angry because he felt the suspension was a personal attack against himself and a direct retaliation led by Captain Dupree and Sergeant LeBlanc.

I dropped Officer Thibodaux off at his house and told him to meet me at our friend's house.

Officer Thibodaux never made it to our friend's house, so we went back to his.

I entered the house, cleared it of all known or unknown assailants and discovered a decapitated body in the living room.

I found blood splatter on the walls and ceilings in the living room and hallway leading to the bedrooms. There was a pool of blood in the master bedroom near the entrance to the bathroom.

Initially, I thought the body was Officer Thibodaux, however once the forensic technician confirmed it was not him, I remembered how it looked.

The body was not fresh. It had already gone through rigor mortis. If that were my friend, his body would have still been warm and had color to its skin. There was something more to this scene.

And I intend to figure out just what that is.

One of which was identified as the headless corpse in Officer Thibodaux's house.

A murder for which he has been framed.

Evidence collected by the Louisiana State Police from inside of Officer Thibodaux's house suggested that he was not responsible for the murder of Samson Tripoli.

Samson's body was staged inside the house. Majority of the blood found inside the house belonged to Officer Thibodaux; too much, in fact, for him to have survived.

His only vehicle was left inside the garage. The keys to his house and car were left in the dish on the side table by the front door.

His cell phone and laptop were left inside the house as well.

There was no blood splatter, drops, or transfer outside of the house to indicate Officer Thibodaux did not leave on his own accord, he was carried out. Likely, in a tarp or other form of plastic.

These men have poisoned our community with the same drugs they were enforcing laws against.

They have bullied and attacked anyone who has threatened their empire which led to Lieutenant Menendez being killed.

Chief Anderson should be held accountable for his death as well.

I want you to understand how difficult this is to write about my friend knowing he is most likely to be dead; killed by men who swore an oath to protect him just as he did.

Officer Thibodaux did not care what a person did, he believed in right and wrong, and helping victims find peace in their suffering.

We owe it to Officer Thibodaux to find and lay him to rest. His murderers, who are also responsible for murdering the other three men, should be brought to justice.

I pray you find favor in my request for intervention and choose to do so.

Godspeed,

William Perry, Deputy Chief

Boiling Point Police Department
1312 Critical Juncture
P.O. Box 1600
Boiling Point, Louisiana 70098
Phone: 318-555-2345
Fax# 225-555-8765

"Have I not commanded you? Be strong and of good courage; do not be afraid, nor be dismayed, for the LORD your God is with you wherever you go."
Joshua 1:9

TO THE HONORABLE

HUMBLY HONORING THE SACRIFICES OF THE MEMBERS OF OUR LAW ENFORCEMENT COMMUNITY WHO CHOOSE TO RESIST CORRUPTION AND STAND FOR WHAT IS RIGHT.

IN MEMORY OF THE FALLEN OFFICERS BOTH CIVIL AND OF THE UNITED STATES ARMED FORCES.

THANK YOU FOR YOUR SERVICE.

ABOUT THE AUTHOR

B. Ash is a DBA for an American author and poet.

He has served in multiple areas of law enforcement as both a deputy sheriff and local police officer as well as a jailer over the course of his extensive law enforcement career.

B. Ash is married and has three children.

www.ingramcontent.com/pod-product-compliance
Lightning Source LLC
Chambersburg PA
CBHW060611310726
48982CB00003B/516

* 9 7 9 8 9 9 2 7 5 4 1 0 0 *